I decide_____ ___go. It was a social
occasio_____lly didn't
expect_____y? Would
you li___

'O_____hing, to feel
his arms _____t that everyone else was looki_____which Duncan
Heyer seemed completely _____

She felt his chin rest for a momen___ __ the top of her
head. She wore her hair loose tonight and as they moved
to the music she was achingly conscious of his firm
masculine figure, the sharp, clean smell of him, the
decisive way he held her, still keeping a hold on her arm
when the music stopped, although she made a move-
ment away.

'Don't go—it will start up again soon—unless you
want to dance with someone else . . .'

'Oh—no,' she said instantly, at which his face broke
into a delighted smile, his eyes searching hers, plumbing
their green-tinted depths.

'Can I call you something other than Staff Nurse?' he
murmured as he took her into his arms again. She could
feel the warmth of him through the softness of her lacy
top and her sheer skirt.

'It's Meryl . . .'

'Yes—it would have to be something like that,' he said
against her ear. 'With those eyes—and you—it's just
right. I like it.'

'I'm glad . . .' she laughed up at him, 'because I can't
change it.'

Now they were oblivious of anyone else on the floor;
close in his arms, moving only to the beat in the throbbing music as if they were the only two people dancing. It
was an embarrassing shock when it stopped suddenly to
find that they weren't and they had to break apart.

Only a few feet away she saw Sister Plumb turn away from another charge sister to whom she had been talking to give Meryl a rather straight, if not entirely disapproving, glance. She didn't look at all pleased and Meryl thought she knew why.

'Oh dear . . .' she murmured, as Duncan bent his head to hear, 'Shouldn't you have asked Sister Plumb to dance? I'm sure she thinks so.'

'Really?' He threw a swift glance in that direction. 'Hmmm—she does look rather fierce. Do I have to?'

'You should,' she spoke reluctantly.

'Well—perhaps later. I'm very happy as I am right now. After this—shall we go and find some food? I'm starving. Lunch was a rather scrappy affair today and I haven't eaten since. Nor have you, I imagine.'

She shook her head. 'No. I didn't either.'

'Come along then.' He steered her away from the floor and in the direction of the buffet room which adjoined; then, depositing her in a chair at a corner table he went off to return with a tray which included wine. It seemed out of character to see him waiting on her and she sat quite still, as he deposited it on the table, desperately trying to control her heartbeats which were hammering away under the lacy top just covering her breasts.

'I brought some Riesling,' he said. 'It seemed the better choice with the chicken, and a kind of Oriental salad. Is this all right?'

'It's fine. I hoped you would choose something light.' She took a sip of wine while he watched her. 'It's nice.'

'Good.' Had he noticed her heightened colour? The tell-tale pulse beating in her throat? Even if his practised eyes did recognise her excitement he might not be conceited enough to think it was because of himself. But then again, he might. He was, she knew now, very male and he was with her because he wanted to be.

It was all so unexpected. Not at all what she had envisaged when she was getting ready for the yearly hospital event. The senior doctors never stayed until the end. In fact, towards midnight it often got a bit noisy, especially among the young doctors and some of the nurses who had left their inhibitions behind. It was supposed to be a fun evening anyway. Duncan, sitting opposite her now, was fully aware of the young, creamy throat above the rounded lace scallops of her evening blouse. The green tints in her eyes seemed to have quite taken over and when they focused on him he found his voice unusually husky, as he asked her about herself and how she came to be there.

'Where are you from, Meryl? London?'

'Cornwall, actually. Don't you detect my West Country accent? Most people do.'

'Yes, now that I think about it. Your family live there?'

He was quick to notice her hesitation and the slight clouding of her eyes before she answered.

'My father died two years ago,' she said quietly, 'after a massive coronary.'

'I'm so sorry . . .'

They both knew and accepted all the implications and he decided not to probe further. But she wanted to put him in the picture with regard to her background.

'My mother died when I was quite small. Seven, to be exact, but she had been in and out of hospital and Dad's sister, who lived quite near, looked after me during holidays and between school times until he picked me up when he left the hospital. He was in administration.

'I see.' He was watching her intently.

'When I was eleven my aunt moved to Scotland. My

uncle worked for a distillery company there. Am I boring you?'

'Of course not. Go on . . .'

She wondered why she was telling him all this, because it was unusual for her to delve back into her childhood; the loneliness she and her father had shared and the ensuing closeness of their relationship.

'My father married Elizabeth that same year,' she went on. 'She was a Sister at the hospital. I liked her from the first moment and it was marvellous to see Dad happy again. She is a lovely person.'

'So—it's all in the family. Nursing.'

'Yes. But that's what we were—a family again. I didn't think of her as a stepmother. I never have; and we're still very close. It was terrible for her when he died. For both of us.'

'Of course. It must have been.' He waited for her to go on; when she didn't he prompted, 'So—you go there when you're on holiday. How I envy you. That lovely rugged coastline and the fishing villages; the white cottages which seem to be all so much a part of Cornwall.'

'Well,' she smiled retrospectively—'we used to live in one right on the harbour, but when Elizabeth was left on her own, because I had already completed my first year's training here, she decided to open a nursing home for elderly people, which meant buying a larger house with a garden, nearer to Falmouth. It was a joint decision because the cottage had to be sold, but it was the best thing in the circumstances. She really needed a project like that to help her over losing my father. It has become home to me now, of course.'

'Will you be going there for Christmas?'

'Oh, yes. I have four days this year. And you? Can you get home?'

'No . . .' He shook his head. 'I'm standing by. Besides, I've just had two whole weeks in Scotland. I think you'd like my part of the world, Meryl, too. The mountains, which cut one down to size, and the valleys which are all a natural sequence running through from the small bunch of straggling grey stone houses where I was born. In the morning and evening it's so beautiful when the mist seems to hover half way between the sky and the foothills. And the colours; the greens and purples and brown, even now, dried heathers. And up there on the tops of the mountains, crisp white snow in contrast. But it's the quiet and the wildness of nature which really gets inside me and gives me time to breathe again. It's up there that I start to think clearly about who I am and where I'm going. A day is enough among the sheep and the quiet magnificence to make me feel completely rejuvenated.'

'I believe it's called communing with nature,' she said as she sat, chin in hand, watching his face, listening; seeing those mountains as he described them, already a picture forming in her mind of his background away from the hospital. But the spell was broken when Jenny and another nurse, accompanied by two young doctors, passed close to their table on the way to the buffet.

'So here you are,' Jenny giggled, raising her eyebrows significantly when she saw who was sitting opposite her. 'I wondered where you were hiding. Good evening, Dr Heyer.'

Duncan inclined his head. 'Nurse Byers, isn't it? Good evening.'

Jenny smirked rather than acknowledged his remark, before moving with her party rather noisily towards the food and drinks bar.

'Your flatmate, I think.'

'Yes.' Reluctantly Meryl recognised that the spell was broken as she was dragged back from the picture he had drawn for her to the rather hilarious scene around them.

Their eyes met ruefully. He was asking if she would like to dance again.

'Not really. It looks very crowded in there now.' He followed her eyes, nodding in agreement. 'Can we escape, do you think? Go somewhere quieter for a coffee or a drink?'

'Oh—yes . . .'

'Why not? He was already standing up, reaching for her. 'We'll get our coats.'

As they left together, Meryl was seemingly regardless but nevertheless very conscious of more than one frankly inquisitive glance in their direction. She felt proud and happy when his arm slid through hers as the door swung behind them. This would certainly cause some gossip, but she didn't care. Only, that the tall Scots doctor at her side was apparently uncaring too. For tonight, at least.

It was strange, walking through the long corridors together to reach the car park where he had left his grey Rover earlier, and emerging to find that a sharp frost was covering everything with a sprinkling of white. She pulled her soft coat around her, turning up the collar which framed her face, as she looked up to where the quiet wards were already dimmed and the night staff preparing for their hours ahead of vigil and crisis, while the machinery of the huge hospital ticked inexorably on, keeping patients breathing, pumping air into oxygen-starved lungs, while others lay helplessly wired up to machines, or the less critical patients were simply drifting into a drugged sleep or lying awake, dreading yet another night in the hospital confines.

'We are the lucky ones,' she said thoughtfully, as she slid into her seat and he fastened his belt beside her. 'We can just drive away and leave it all to someone else tonight.'

'We're not that insensitive though, are we? I don't find it especially easy simply to switch off, and I don't think that you do either.'

'No . . .' she smiled ruefully. 'It's a way of life, isn't it?'

He brought the car to a stop as an ambulance turned into the precinct, with blue lights flashing, and swiftly drove up the slope to the Casualty section. Doors slid back and the wheels of an emergency admittance were set in motion.

Duncan drew a deep breath as the car moved forward into the roadway. 'There goes another human being in dire distress,' he muttered. 'But life has many guises and tonight is ours, Meryl. Now, where would you like to go?' He glanced at the watch on his wrist, just visible beneath the white cuffs of his shirt. She never knew why the wide leather strap and his masculine wrist should have an immediate effect on her the way they did.

He hadn't realised it was quite so late. 'I'm afraid the pubs will be closing soon,' he told her, 'it's almost ten-thirty. We could drive out to a country club I know or, another suggestion, my flat is quite near. My coffee comes fully recommended. Unless you prefer to be taken home. It's your choice, Meryl.'

'Home . . .' she teased, 'is right back from where we have just come. I did tell you that Jenny and I share a flat in the Radway Block.'

'So you did. I—just wasn't quite sure where that is, you see.'

Should she believe him? And wasn't she very curious to see his flat? The idea jelled and became exciting. After all, he wasn't a stranger. It had to be all right where he was concerned.

'Can we go back to your place?' she asked tentatively. 'I'd like that.'

'Of course. I've said so.' He went on, as the car switched to the inner lane, 'I don't want to lose you yet. Heaven knows when an opportunity like this will occur again. Besides, it's become a somewhat unexpected evening, hasn't it?' He threw her a swift glance. 'Anything can happen when the Gods are in this mood—as the folk at home would tell you. Even the mountains have moods, you know.'

'But we aren't in Scotland,' she observed, reciprocating his teasing smile.

'Don't you think I know that?'

All her feminine wiles were aroused now. She sat very still, pursing her lips. His tone had been like a caress. Exciting undertones were making a new pulsating in her throat and she was now very aware of the intimacy inside the close confines of the car as his long legs pushed forward and the clean, masculine scent of his warm skin sent a mysterious power over her body which was almost magnetic. She was momentarily at a loss for words.

But he was turning into a gravel drive and stopping at the entrance to what, she thought, was a rather exclusive three-storied block of flats.

When they were inside he took her elbow and led her towards the stairs. 'I'm afraid I don't have the penthouse suite,' he told her as they went up together, 'but I do have a good view over the gardens at the back.'

She got the impression that he was proud of having his own place and wanted her to see it. But while she waited for him to insert his key in the lock a thought burst into her mind. And, as they went into the tiny hall, she came straight out with it, looking up into his face when she said firmly, 'I'm not in the habit of doing this. I—just wanted you to know that. In fact—I can't think of anyone else I would have . . . Do you think I'm terribly naive?'

'Of course not,' he grinned openly. 'Let's forget all that, shall we? Come along in—this, as you see, is my living room—and there is the kitchen—not large, but adequate—the bathroom, and where I sleep . . .'

He indicated another door through which she glimpsed a single divan and built-in white furniture, in contrast to a dark brown carpet and curtains, clean and masculine.

Here too, in the lounge, she was pleasantly surprised at his decor as she slid out of her coat.

'Sit down. I'll get some coffee under way. I expect you'd like a brandy with it. Do sit down, Meryl. You look—apprehensive—and I hoped you wouldn't be.'

He disappeared into the small kitchen and she could hear cupboards being opened and sounds of activity while she sank into the softness of a dark green velvet settee, revelling in the warmth of the electric fire he had switched on when they came in.

'Oh—this is nice . . .' she said appreciatively when he came back with two brandy glasses. 'What a lovely evening it's been.'

'That should be my line,' he began, looking down at her. 'I had no idea when I started out from here earlier that I was going to have you all to myself.' He smiled gently, his head to one side as he regarded her. 'One dance, if you're lucky, Duncan old chap—is all you can expect—I told myself, and look what I've ended up with. A lovely girl, so different from that still lovely but prim staff nurse in the blue print dress and purple-belted waist, flat shoes and a determined walk which keeps my mind very much on my work when it sometimes wants to simply take off.'

'What a long speech,' she laughed with him. Not for

anything would she confess to her own reactions when he was around.

'The coffee . . .' they both shouted at once as the delicious aroma of it burst into the room. 'Shall I come and help?' she called as he disappeared.

'If you like.'

Perhaps because the space was so limited that they were almost touching anyway, or because their eyes found each other's at the same moment—when she turned from putting the cups on a tray—it was by a mutual need that his hands moved to her elbows and he was drawing her to him.

Meryl held her breath as his mouth came closer. She couldn't bear it if he didn't kiss her now; so he found her lips waiting, already parting instinctively for the firmness of his. Duncan was very strongly male and his kiss positive and devastatingly thorough, so that she was trembling when at last they broke away from each other.

Duncan's voice was unsteady when he said huskily, 'Oh, Meryl—do you know what you're doing to me?'

Her face was flushed when she looked up at him, to be pulled passionately into his arms again. She whispered against his neck shyly, 'I—think so . . .' and then his lips, warm against her own, were teasingly evoking a dormant sweetness in her pliant body that she had not known could happen. Her arms went up around the back of his neck where the brown hair grew thickly. How often she had wanted to touch it when he bent over the desk or even a patient. It had always attracted her strangely, and now . . .

But, quite abruptly, he was resolutely pulling her away from him, pushing back his tousled hair while she stood a little apart wonderingly.

But he spoke gently when he told her to, 'Go and wait for me to bring in the coffee. Fortunately, this new machine thing keeps it hot. My latest acquisition—as you see—I'm getting quite house-proud, for a bachelor. Please go in there, Meryl.'

He was talking to recover something of his self-possession, of course. She knew as she turned to do as he asked that he too had been unprepared for their immediate rapport.

When he came in with the tray and more brandy he stood for a moment looking down at her quizzically, while her eyes, which in her case really did mirror her thoughts, went unerringly to his. He took a deep breath before sitting down next to her. 'After this,' he said sternly, 'I'm going to take you back. It's not what I want . . .' he went on, reaching to pick up her coffee cup and pass it to her—'but—I think we both need time to—recover, if that's the word.' He grinned boyishly. 'That was rather like going in at the deep end when you're not a very strong swimmer. Because—I hadn't realised what a very lovely woman you are, Meryl. And I don't wholly trust myself tonight. Besides all that—it is quite late and I know you have to be on duty by eight while I am in theatre from eight-thirty. And—I have quite a formidable list tomorrow.'

'You're making excuses,' she said gently, while her lips curved with a tremulous smile.

'Reasons . . .' he intervened. 'Brandy?'

She took the glass from his fingers. 'Thank you . . .' she hesitated.

'Duncan—the name is Duncan—when we're alone. And there will be more times—when we are, Meryl. There have to be,' he interposed.

'When I come back from Cornwall, perhaps?' she began tentatively.

'Yes. When will that be?'

'Two days after Christmas.'

'And you're off?'

'The day after tomorrow.'

He stood up, resolutely picking up her coat from the chair where she had thrown it when they came in, holding it for her while she slipped into it. She felt his mouth brush the back of her neck lightly, shivering deliciously but knowing that she must not turn into his arms again. He was trying to avoid that so she must go along with it.

'I love your dress,' he said as he bent to pick up her bag. 'Very feminine—just as I like my women to look. I was extremely proud to be with you tonight. Any man would have . . .'

'And I you,' she said at once.

He looked puzzled. 'I don't quite understand your complete honesty. Or is it naivety? No—that can't be. You see, my experience has been that most women are, on the whole, a devious species and I have learned to tread warily. I would never again allow any woman to use me, but you are deceptively different. Just a warning voice somewhere . . .'

She was shocked and a little angry as she went with him into the hall, pondering over his words. What on earth prompted them? And what exactly did he mean?

'You've obviously been let down quite badly at some time,' she commented drily. 'Surely to be completely honest and able to trust each other is the first criterion in any relationship. I had no idea you were quite so biased.'

They spoke little on the way back to the hospital. She felt oddly disappointed and smarting at the arrogance behind his remarks. He stopped the car a little distance away from Radway Block, against one of the trees which lined the access road. There was a light on in their apartment.

'Jenny seems to be up still,' she said coolly.

He leaned forward to look up at the window. 'It is after midnight.'

'I know. I must go. Thank you for . . .' There was a definite finality in her voice.

He gave a little groan. 'Oh—Meryl—do forgive me. I must have sounded a bumptious ass back there. I'm afraid I'm not a very diplomatic guy. I just got the impression that you were expecting me to—and—oh— God—don't you see? I wanted to make love to you quite desperately tonight.' He took her unyielding face into both hands, 'but it's become so much more than that. I think I'm falling in love with you.'

Her eyes were shining in the half light now and as his hands slipped behind her hair, drawing her face close to his, she suddenly understood, scarcely able to believe that he had actually admitted that he was falling in love, just as she was with him.

There were bright tears in her eyes before she closed them as his mouth came to find hers; moving gently before it captured her warm parted lips in a very positive way, taking her beyond anything she had ever experienced in a kiss before.

She pushed him firmly away when it was over, her voice tremulous, breathlessly happy, as she touched his lips with her finger, tracing his mouth gently.

'Goodnight,' she whispered.

'I must see you again soon,' he muttered.

'Tomorrow perhaps. But not alone, I'm afraid. So— not until I come back from Cornwall.'

'Which is a very frustrating thought—to say the least.'

She laughed softly. 'Goodnight—it's been a wonderful evening.'

'Yes . . .' he said softly—'hasn't it?'

Then she was running across the concrete slabs towards the nurses' block, shivering as the frosty air invaded her coat; then into the warmth of the building. Running lightly up the stairs and letting herself into the lighted apartment. Jenny was asleep, her door firmly closed for which Meryl was grateful. When she crossed to the window and looked down the car had gone.

CHAPTER THREE

MERYL sensed an undercurrent of mixed curiosity among the nurses on D-level next morning. The patients, though, responded to the unmistakable glow of quiet happiness which showed in her eyes, her confident walk and new assurance in her manner as she began her work.

Last night, before she slept, she had re-lived those last minutes with Duncan, finding the joy of it almost unbearable. What miracle had happened that he had actually admitted that he was in love with her? From a man she hadn't thought could be in the least bit romantic, nor impulsive—yet the words had burst from his lips as if he couldn't hold them back and became extra precious because she had glimpsed his vulnerability where she was concerned. Now—she only wanted to see him again, if only for a few moments. A brief glance, with a secret message for her, would renew the wonder of it all. But it was highly improbable today. Even now, she had a mental picture of him, hidden beneath his green gown and mask, oblivious of everything and everyone but the patient he was working on at that precise moment.

There were a few teasing remarks from the others on duty with her that morning, but she knew how to switch them off and had always discouraged gossip about anyone on the hospital staff, as they knew.

But Sister Plumb was another matter. She was a little distant right from the start, but she waited until they were alone at the desk before she said, eyeing her staff nurse keenly,

'There's no need to ask if you enjoyed your evening, is there? You quite appropriated our Dr Heyer. I've never seen the man so bemused. Everyone noticed, and that you both left early. What were you trying to do? Set the tongues wagging? A little indiscreet, surely.'

'I don't think it concerns anyone else, Sister,' Meryl said quietly, 'nor do I have to explain why we left early. I had a lovely evening though. Did you?'

'Oh . . .' Sister Plumb shrugged, a little put out by Meryl's reticence but, as the senior member of her staff knew, hardly able to continue in the same vein, 'it's the usual knees-up every year, isn't it? The younger ones making fools of themselves and the rest looking on. I don't know why I bother to go. Some of the doctors' wives just stand around in groups making bitchy remarks. They don't fraternise, and they were probably in the nursing profession before they hooked their husbands anyway. Your lace blouse was a bit daring, I thought. And did you shorten last year's skirt? It wasn't new, was it?'

'My black chiffon—yes—I took a few inches off the bottom,' Meryl said happily. 'It only gets worn a couple of times in a year and I still like it.'

She looked down at the fob watch on her dress, curbing the rush of resentful feelings which threatened. She had expected some caustic remarks, but not phrased with such subtlety. But now the subject was closed.

'I'll go and see the boy in Ward Three,' she said quietly. 'He's very apprehensive about going to theatre. Eleven, you said, Sister?'

The starched cap, worn with a navy dress and white collar, bent over the list. 'Nigel Blair. Yes. Nurse Jeans can go with him. Then Mr Pratt and the hip replacement later, because Mr Williams is doing that. I shall be off this afternoon, but they will probably all stay in Recovery; so it's just routine. Oh—Miss Beard—for X-Rays this morning. They'll take her on her bed, of course. So . . .' she pursed her lips tightly, 'better go to it then. It looks like being one of those days . . .'

And Meryl, already on her way down the corridor, was inclined to agree with her. It did become a hectic morning. By lunch time her back was aching because there is nothing worse than constant bending over beds to strain the support muscles. The sheer exertion of hoisting patients up on to pillows, or getting them bodily out into wheelchairs, supervising drip feeds, administering drugs, all with one eye on the clock and the other on the nurses in training, which meant that because she was responsible and knew how, she often worked much harder than they.

Over a snatched lunch she wondered if Duncan was getting a few snide glances too. She knew what some of the surgeons were like, behind the scenes as it were. One heard some very earthy remarks, even in the process of taking someone's limbs apart and replacing them with plastic. All in a day's work. Would she see him before she left for Cornwall? Four whole days seemed an eternity. She had to go, of course.

At five, Sister returned, releasing her for two hours during which time she was supposed to have a meal and relax, to be back at seven, preparing patients for the night staff to take over after the bell rang for visitors to leave at eight.

Duncan had not, as yet, been up to the wards. Sometimes he paid a fleeting visit to a patient he was concerned about and she had hoped he might do so today. Surely he wasn't still in theatre?

As she left the dining-room her pulses reacted the moment she caught sight of him. He was with Mr Williams and was obviously ready to leave. Standing back to let the consultant surgeon precede him into the lift, he saw her coming, excused himself and waited until the lift doors had closed behind the other man. The light above his head caught a streak of red in the brown hair which looked as if he had just had a shower, soft and still slightly damp, and her whole body seemed to go out to him because of the tiredness around his eyes. Except that now they leapt into life and there was nothing forced about the smile of real pleasure he gave her.

'I've been wondering if I'd see you,' he said, glancing around to make sure they were alone briefly.

'And I you . . . Did you have a long list?'

He shrugged. 'A difficult one. What time will you be free tonight? Or do you have things to do if you're leaving early in the morning?'

'I'm very organised actually . . .' She raised her eyes to his quickly because people were leaving the lifts and passing constantly.

'At nine then? Come down when you see the car. Just for an hour.'

'Yes,' she said, not caring who saw her contained happiness now as she dived into the lift and left him standing there.

Sister had been inundated with anxious relatives waiting to speak to her and was only too glad to hand over to Meryl who had to detail a junior staff nurse to organise the duties for the next hour after that.

But at last she was free and now her mind ran on to re-shuffle her own evening. She still had some Christmas gifts to wrap, but her bag was already packed with only a few last-minute additions. Sister had left a small present on her desk addressed to herself, together with a card which said, 'Have a good holiday'. So Meryl breathed more easily because that was the first time today that Sister had mentioned that she would be away from tomorrow. Yet, her deputy was already laid on and she had known for days.

Jenny was in the bathroom washing her hair when Meryl put her key in the lock and went into the tiny hall, glancing at more cards for herself on the telephone table; but she came into the kitchen, her hair wrapped in a towel and plugged in the kettle for coffee.

'Thank goodness we aren't going out tonight. Bed for me early. I'm whacked. Lucky you—home for Christmas.'

'Yes. I'm looking forward to a break. I really need to get away.'

'Oh? I thought it might be different now. Can you bear to leave Dr Heyer?'

'That . . .' Meryl said sternly, 'is a taboo subject. Even for you.'

Jenny giggled. 'You're not going to live last night down easily, you know. Everyone saw you together all evening.'

'Coffee?' Meryl said pointedly, passing her cup and taking her own into the bathroom, determined to switch off.

'Point taken,' Jenny called after her with her tongue in her cheek. 'They're forecasting snow by the end of the week, did you know? Suppose you can't get back?'

'I'll get back. Somehow.'

'I'll bet you will,' she murmured provokingly. But by then Meryl had turned on the taps and closed the door.

Coming back fifteen minutes later wearing a white roll-neck sweater and pleated skirt was bound to provoke more comment from Jenny, experimenting with some heated curlers in the lounge, but stopping to gape at Meryl curiously when she saw that she was dressed.

'You're not going out?'

'Yes.'

'Where?'

'I'm not sure, yet.'

'Oh—come on. You must know.'

'Well . . .' The entry-phone bleeped in the hall, rescuing her. As she picked it up she heard his delicious Scots brogue in answer to her 'Meryl Summers here.'

'I'm waiting by the gate,' he reminded her.

'Oh—I'll be right down.'

'Good . . .'

Jenny raised quizzical eyebrows as she hurriedly pulled on her coat. 'Dr Heyer—I presume?'

'Right first time. I won't be late.'

'Oh, yes?' the other girl teased.

'I do have a train to catch in the morning,' Meryl reminded her. 'And those curlers are too hot.'

Leaving her flatmate to cope with a strand of scorched hair, she closed the door and ran excitedly down the stairs and out into the frosty night. Her aching back and tired muscles had disappeared and as Duncan leaned across and opened her door when he saw her coming, only the pleasure of seeing him again was paramount.

'I'm being selfish,' he said with a grin, showing his strong white teeth in the dusky night, 'but I'm adept at getting what I want.' He pressed her hand in an impulsive gesture. 'Lovely to see you—have you to myself for a short while, Meryl. Shall we go to the Fox and Hounds; maybe find a corner where we can be together, if not alone? At least it will be warm there and as we don't have unlimited time . . .'

'Fine,' she murmured, not caring where he took her, just as long as they were together.

He too had changed into a cream roll-necked sweater with cords and a brown velvet jacket. Why had she thought his taste in clothes might be more conventional?

After all, she had only ever seen him in dark suits or white coats or green theatre garb. Her heartbeats accelerated when he put his arm quickly around her neck, turning her face to his, kissing her with a warmth of passion which blocked everything else outside her conscious thought. And when he let her go and, drawing a deep breath, his hands returned to the wheel, she heard her own breath escape weakly on a long sigh of tightened emotion.

'You see?' he said huskily. 'This is only the beginning for us. My dear girl—you make me feel nineteen again. I'm going to hate to let you out of my sight, even for four days. But, I promise you, tonight I shall keep my distance. We'll just go somewhere and talk.'

'The Fox and Hounds, you said.'

'That's right. Though—this coming up to the Christmas period is always a busy one there.'

'I don't mind.'

His promise to keep his distance tonight was something she appreciated. She wanted very much to get to know him first as a person. Up until now she knew only what she had seen of the professional man, and last night, of course. And although she knew that he had made her recognise the dormant passion within herself for what it was, just waiting to be released, and that he was also aware of her instant response to his male approach, recognising the flow of chemistry between them and a growing need, she didn't want it all to move so quickly towards an uncontrollable situation where only physical sensations were paramount.

Of course, what she didn't realise was that because of their medical background they were half way there already. But tonight he wanted to talk shop, though only for a little while. Perhaps because he knew she would understand the pressures inside the theatre walls, and he hadn't been able to shut off completely. Not quite. So he told her about the corrective bone surgery they had done that day on a boy from one of the local schools. 'It's not something to be hurried, but when and if it works it is extremely good for one's ego. And the whole reasoning behind choosing this profession, as you know. Oh, Meryl—there's such a long way to go. And with new technology and new insight—and experience—it's getting very exciting.'

He rose then to fetch her another glass of wine but, she noticed, making his own small whisky, unadulterated, last. When he came back he watched her face, concentrating his gaze on her eyes and mouth as she told him about the nursing home and what her Christmas was going to be like.

Then, quite suddenly, he leaned forward, grasping her hand. 'Shall we go?' he asked urgently.

She drained her glass, wondering why he hadn't noticed she still had some wine left. But when they reached the door she saw that two of the younger doctors had just come in with the two nurses they had been with the previous night. Oh, dear—was it always to be like this? she wondered, stifling a sigh. And did he really mind so much? Was it for her sake or for his, this trying to avoid hospital gossip? Surely their private lives were their own?

But, with his hand possessively under her elbow, it didn't seem that he minded too much. And maybe they weren't even noticed. She was being much too critical.

Outside the icy wind hit them. 'Oh . . .' she shivered, feeling his arm go round her then. 'I do hope this doesn't end with snow. It smells a bit like it.'

'I don't think so. You're a true girl of the sea, aren't you? Snow in the wind; except that it's coming from the opposite direction.'

'That's what I mean,' she laughed softly. 'And if I get snowbound, I won't be able to get back. I suppose for such a short time I shouldn't consider a longish journey.'

'No . . .' he agreed, his mouth quivering slightly in a half smile. 'I don't think you should go . . .'

As the car moved forward his hand found hers in her lap, covering it with strong fingers which, in itself, brought reactions from her in a fusion of oneness.

'Nothing will ever seem the same again,' he admitted. 'You've walked right into my life now, haven't you?'

'But I'm only just on the fringe of it,' she murmured, throwing him a teasing glance.

'Ah—that's what you think. I'm hoping that you're here to stay.'

A rush of sheer happiness enveloped her, bringing a dreamy look to her eyes, but Duncan was already on a more practical wavelength and with an effort she responded when he asked what time her train got in on Friday.

'I really don't know. Around six, I think. That's usually the time.'

'Well—have a good rest. You've earned it. No doubt you'll come back to a ward full of Christmas casualties,' he said realistically as the car sped up the hill and stopped on the roadway outside the main entrance to the hospital.

'You are parked on a double yellow line,' she reminded him.

'I know. Which means I don't intend to keep you out any longer, thus removing the temptation.' Turning, he reached into the back seat, releasing the warm scent of his body; male and sharply clean—a close, personal contact which was still so new to her it brought a rush of colour to her face. But he didn't notice, as turning, he put a gift-wrapped parcel into her lap. 'Just some choco-lates,' he said—'and here are a couple of magazines for the journey tomorrow. And—I'll be thinking about you at odd moments through the day and, selfishly, I'm glad it isn't any longer than four days. Goodnight, Meryl. Safe journey.'

He kissed her firmly while her lips tremulously parted under his, but tonight Duncan was in complete control and, except to mutter huskily, 'Oh—my dear girl—what you do to me . . .' as he let her go, and pushing a strand of her silky, newly-washed hair from her eyes—he didn't weaken. Then, as a police car drove by, he leaned across to open the door for her.

'Happy Christmas,' he let go of her hand reluctantly. 'Four days is really going to seem one hell of a time,' he declared flatly.

There was a suggestion of feminine witchery in her smile as he leaned forward and looked up at her.

'Happy Christmas,' she said softly, knowing that she would think of his words often while they were apart. And he had meant them.

The train journey seemed endless, but at last the familiar landmarks began to appear on the landscape. The tall white slag heaps of the clay mines and sweep of green fields and distant hills. She began to gather her things together, grateful for the magazines which, being the more expensive ones, she seldom saw, and the articles and fashion pages had a new fascination for her now because she was in love and she wanted to look good and wear attractive clothes for Duncan, whom she knew appreciated good taste. His solicitude had touched her. She didn't often have presents and as she reached for her gloves the exhilaration of going back to him again soon brought a fresh surge of happiness, as she gazed out of the window and saw the spires and chimneys of the small town just ahead.

The taxi sped up and away from the traffic and the Christmas shoppers, and on the top of the hill, in a quiet avenue, put her down outside 'Bay Trees—a Home for the Elderly', as the white notice in the garden described it. Two scented bay trees stood, one on each side of the white gate, and the white door with black iron markings was already opening to release Elizabeth, running to meet her, to hug her with genuine pleasure. 'Oh—it's lovely to have you home again.'

'And to be here,' Meryl laughed, feeling like a school-girl coming home from boarding school for the holidays, and not at all like the competent, responsible senior staff nurse, which was her other image.

Inside, a tall Christmas tree dominated one corner of the square hall, its lights gaily colourful, and the dark red carpet warm and welcoming, as she followed her step-mother up the wide staircase to her own apartments. An electric fire flickered in the hearth and here the Christmas cards and a red poinsettia gave the room colour and a festiveness. A lovely pink cyclamen on a corner table caught Meryl's admiration.

'Oh—isn't that beautiful. A present?'

Elizabeth blushed. 'Yes—actually, one of the visiting doctors brought it in yesterday.'

'How delightful . . .' She didn't comment on the writing on the card which said simply, 'For You,'—neither had her stepmother's blush escaped her. So—why not? Perhaps later, when they were together quiet-ly, she might tell her about Duncan. But now—she just wanted to change into something comfortable and relax and talk.

'I'll make some tea—or would you prefer coffee?'

Elizabeth asked. 'I've prepared some sandwiches. I thought we might eat later.'

'I'd love tea. It seems very quiet downstairs; don't you have many patients?'

'Three have gone to stay out for a night or two, but there are still eight who will be here with us. They're mostly having an after-lunch nap. You know your room, my dear. Nothing's changed. I'll have the tea in here ready for you. Don't be long.'

'No staff problems?' Meryl asked curiously, when they were sitting together that evening after an excellent meal.

'Not really.' Elizabeth put down her coffee cup and crossed her slim legs. It struck Meryl quite forcibly how attractive she looked. A new, softer hairstyle, framed a sensitive, oval face and she really had the loveliest brown eyes. Meryl had never known her age exactly. Suddenly she wanted to tell her about Duncan. Which reminded her of the unopened box of chocolates still in her bag.

'I've got something for us,' she told her. 'Wait just one moment.' It was a link with him, as she took the ribbon-wrapped parcel back into the lounge, undoing it while Elizabeth looked on with interest, gasping when she saw the hand-made chocolates displayed invitingly inside.

'They look gorgeous . . .'

'Duncan Heyer gave them to me,' Meryl said with pride. 'He's the senior ortho surgeon, and, rather nice . . .'

'So it seems. Is this a thank-you present or are they supposed to mean something more? You haven't mentioned him before. What is he like?'

'He's nice . . .' Meryl said with the kind of far-off smile Elizabeth understood, while she waited for more.

'We were both at the Christmas do the other evening. Well—two nights ago actually, and—we left together. It all started from there, which started a few tongues wagging.

'I'll bet. Is it serious?'

'It—could be. Yes—I think it is.'

'Good for you—it's time you had someone of your own. How old is he?' She looked anxious. 'Not too old, I hope.'

Meryl laughed softly. 'No—of course not. I don't really know. In his thirties, I should think. He's very much the broad Scot—one doesn't tread on his toes. I used to think he was rather arrogant when I watched him in theatre. But I think it's a kind of self-assurance, where his work is concerned. He's terribly meticulous—and not above showing it if he's annoyed. Which isn't very often. I—didn't dream we would ever go out together though.

'Why not? You're a very attractive girl and he's probably been admiring you from a distance as well. But—don't fall in too deeply, too quickly, Meryl. Until you're sure he really means it. I've seen it happen so often—I'd hate to see you hurt.'

'It—isn't like that,' Meryl interrupted.

'No,' Elizabeth said wryly, 'it never is. But I must say he has very good taste in chocolates, and I'd say it looks very hopeful from where I'm sitting. Now—excuse me for a short time. I'll just go and say goodnight to them all. I think the last of the visitors have gone now.'

Meryl leaned back in the chair and let her thoughts drift back to Duncan. It was easier to see it all in focus when one was away from a situation and tonight she seemed very far away. It was lovely to be here with her stepmother because, of course, some of the personal things from her old home had come here too and her father's photograph on a side table brought him closer also. But tonight home seemed to be back there, where Duncan was, and she was feeling a little bereft without him.

Closing her eyes, she could imagine the texture of his face against her own; the deep pulsating excitement his kisses aroused; the strength of his hand holding firmly to hers. Oh—she loved those hands of the man who said he was in love with her.

Already she knew that this was what she had been waiting for. This, the reality of love as she wanted it to be. Just a beginning of what could be between them. So wonderful; starting from sheer hero worship carefully hidden from everyone else, to that flare of passion, the moment they were alone, where no prying eyes could see; when she had glimpsed the man needing her love and she had trembled in his arms, wanting to meet that need. Of course, it was all too soon. That wasn't the way she expected it to be at all. One didn't just rush in and spoil everything. It was not the way to assuage the yearning hunger his kisses started, the moment his lips touched hers, either. Not for her.

Next day, being Christmas Eve, Meryl and her step-mother drove into town for some last-minute shopping. She bought a tiny figurine for Elizabeth and a silver St Christopher which she planned to give to Duncan on her return. This was only after some deliberation. Perhaps it was too soon. She still felt a little out of depth where he was concerned. It was the hospital situation, of course, and because he was hierarchy on D-Level, while she was still just one of the nursing brigade, ready to do his command. It wasn't going to be easy to adjust to this set difference between them either. Perhaps it should be for him to break it down. So that they were both exactly on the same level, as a man and a woman in love. But hadn't he already started to do that? So how would he continue when she got back? The next time they were together? Oh—she couldn't wait. Friday seemed an eternity away.

Christmas Day brought its own special pleasure. In the morning there were carols from the nearby church choristers in front of the tree which brought a few tears from the old people who recalled other family Christmases, but had now to accept the fact that they themselves needed nursing care and looking after. Then the presents, piled around the tree. Then the traditional lunch for everyone and visitors and treats all round. It was a good day in spite of, or even because of, the nostalgia and, tired out, they were all asleep early, both Meryl and Elizabeth helping out to lighten the work load. When the night nurse arrived, punctual as ever, they were able to entertain a few close friends in the upstairs lounge who, like themselves, were happy to just sit around and talk.

On Boxing Day morning they were both invited out for drinks, but Elizabeth was on duty all afternoon so that her part-time nurse could be with her children. Meryl decided on a brisk walk down to the bay and along the sea road. It was cold, but amazingly the sun shone through in a blue and white sky, glinting on the white-tipped waves far out to sea. She didn't feel she had been home if she missed seeing the bay again; memories came flooding back as she remembered the other times. Swimming with her father through the long summers; sun-drenched sands and holidaymakers; and going back together to their little cottage around the headland. She couldn't bring herself to go that far on this blustery winter day, but retraced her steps up the winding path towards the avenue of trees to the Home, quietly happy at the prospect of tomorrow's journey back to the hospital and Duncan. She wouldn't see him probably until the weekend, but he just might phone. And he would know that she was back by evening.

When the taxi came for her next day, Elizabeth made her promise to let her know how things progressed.

'Of course I will.'

'I wish I could have run you to the station, but I've asked the doctor to come and see Mr Gregory. I'm a bit concerned about him.'

'Is he—*the* doctor?' Meryl asked innocently.

'Oh, no . . .' Elizabeth had fallen into the trap. 'It's Dr Jason—sixty; and gruff with it. Like a cuddly bear, but the old people love him. Now—do phone sometimes, Meryl—you are all my family, you know.'

'I know . . .' she answered gently. 'It's been a lovely Christmas and, thanks to you, a real break.'

Hours later and after a most frustrating journey because, of course, there was only a skeleton service on the railways, a fact which Meryl had overlooked, the train drew into Salisbury Station and the guard was shouting, 'All change, please.'

'Oh, no . . .' she groaned, meeting the blue eyes of a fellow passenger sitting opposite, who promptly swore. 'It's supposed to go right through.'

'Well . . .' he said resignedly, 'there's not much we can do about it. Come on—maybe there's time for a cup of coffee. I see the buffet bar is open.' He was grinning broadly now.

There was time. A whole forty minutes; so it seemed perfectly natural to go into the buffet together.

'I've been spending Christmas with my parents who live the other side of Exeter,' he told her, 'but I have to be on duty early tomorrow. I'm a policeman.'

Meryl told him that she also must report for duty in the morning.

'Now—with those eyes and your looks I should have thought your job was something quite glamorous,' he said, passing her the sugar.

'Well—you're quite wrong,' she retorted laughingly. 'There's nothing glamorous about nursing, I can assure you. Rewarding, yes—but glamorous—no.'

'I see what you mean. I'm often up at the Royal. Is that where you are?'

She nodded.

'Which department?'

'Orthopaedics—at the moment.'

Their conversation cheered up the last part of the journey and they were on quite easy terms when the train drew into the lighted station.

He reached for her bags from the rack and opened the door, jumping down on to the platform behind her.

As they walked to the exit he assumed an attentive, rather proprietory manner towards Meryl, guiding her between the other passengers, then saying something which made her smile up at him delightedly, giving quite the wrong impression to Dr Heyer who had spent the last three hours waiting at the station for her.

Now he took a step backwards into the shadows. He never knew why for, of course, he should have come forward to meet her when she would have run into his arms, overjoyed to see him there.

Instead, her delight and relief, especially when she saw the long queue for the taxis, already non-existent, was because her policeman had offered her a lift in his Ford car, parked behind the station. Right up to the hospital.

Duncan stood quite still, watching her go with him and waiting while he unlocked it, he saw her get in and drive away. Only then did he walk towards the grey Rover in which he had spent long hours, just waiting, but it hadn't mattered, then. Now he was disappointed and angry. Disappointed with Meryl, but the anger was directed towards himself.

CHAPTER FOUR

BACK on familiar territory the following morning Meryl found, as she expected, that there had been several changes in the wards. New admissions over the Christmas holiday had necessitated a general switching round of some beds, and it took her a short while to familiarise herself with the new set-up.

She wondered, as she drew the curtains back from a bed, if and when she would see Duncan and decided to look at the rota list, ascertaining, to her delight, that he was on call today. Which meant that any emergency operation needing more than routine surgery in his field would bring him into the hospital. She still prickled with slight disappointment that he hadn't phoned her last night. But she could just as easily have phoned him. So why hadn't she? Except that she hadn't—yet.

Now she wanted to be reassured. Just a glimpse of his white-coated figure, a swift look from those deeply set eyes, would be enough.

Returning after a quick snack lunch her eyes scanned the doctors' car park for his grey Rover, but it wasn't there. Oh, well, tonight he would be sure to call her, but he might not realise she could be later than usual.

About to cross the exit road, she looked right and left, waiting while a police car, which had obviously accompanied the ambulance still outside Casualty, came to a stop at the kerb and her rail co-passenger from last night jumped out, coming round the front of the car to her.

'Hullo, there. I wondered if I'd see you,' he said without preamble, his lop-sided grin much in evidence as he pushed his hat a little to the back of his head and stood quite close to her. 'Gee—what a morning; were you thrown in at the deep end too?'

'Something like that,' she agreed, thinking how impressive he looked in his uniform. 'It was such a help getting that lift home last night. I'm very grateful.'

'So—when are you going to show how grateful you are, then? I want to see you again—you know that.'

'Oh—I don't think I can, you see . . .'

'I know. There's this doctor . . . So, why didn't he meet your train last night?'

'I don't know. The trains were rather unpredictable and we didn't arrange anything. I'm—sorry . . .' She glanced at the fob watch on her dress beneath the cloak she wore. 'Oh—heavens, I must go—Sister is waiting to go off.'

Inside the car the radio bleeped and his co-officer let down the window, beckoning to him urgently.

His hand gripped her arm. 'I don't give up that easily, you know. You'll see me around—and you look quite super in your uniform.' His wide smile was a promise. The car shot forward with blue lights flashing; and she ran across the paved gardens to the doors of West Wing.

She didn't see the grey Rover which had edged into the only available space in the far corner of the parking lot. But as Duncan got out and turned to lock the door, his eyes were drawn to the uniformed figure of the girl he loved, in close conversation with the police officer beside the white patrol car, recognising him as the man she had arrived with last evening.

He was certainly a good looker, in an athletic kind of way, and behaving rather possessively too, with his hand on her arm, considering they had only met for the first time yesterday. If that was true. And, if not, why hadn't Meryl told him about this other man who seemed to know more about her movements than he did?

Deliberately, he went in through Casualty, knowing that she would enter through the butterfly doors into the corridor closer to the staff cloakroom in the other wing.

Just that one incident, of seeing her with the same man in so short a time, had added fuel to the smouldering fires of his jealousy. And how was Meryl to know that jealousy had broken the only other real romance of his life? That had been when he was a junior registrar at his London hospital. Now he felt the same seething disruption within himself and an annoyance which caused a frown to furrow his forehead as he went quickly through to his room. Annoyance, because this time he was older and should be wiser and know how to combat this weakness, if that was what it was. But, in consequence, he felt even more intense about Meryl because he knew now how much he wanted her. He had thought that he had found the one girl he could trust beyond all doubt. Then an urgent summons from Casualty shut out everything other than the present emergency, needing immediate decisions, as he prepared for theatre.

Just after four o'clock, Meryl picked up the internal phone on her desk, answering it in her normal, caring voice, coming from long months of learning how to shut off from one situation to another.

It was Theatre Sister. 'We've got a patient for you, or will have when he's ready. Dr Heyer wants a word.'

Her heart leapt. So he was in the hospital. Then his voice, clipped and efficient, 'Sister Plumb?'

'No. Staff Nurse here. Sister is off duty, Dr Heyer.'

'Oh. I think I'd better come up myself,' he finished abruptly.

She replaced the receiver, feeling a little deflated, the joy surging through her at hearing his voice quashed by an undertone, a little unexpected. But he had just come from theatre and she knew that Sister would be around, within earshot, if he had phoned from her office. But— she would see him in a few minutes. Putting down her pen, with which she had been entering notes on a patient's record card, she got up and automatically straightened her cap, pushing back a soft wave of hair and then smoothing down her dress, finding that her hands were trembling just a fraction as she automatically tidied the papers on the desk, listening for the sound of closing lift doors. Heavens—she reprimanded herself— this had to stop. Why did she have this feeling that something was wrong—changed—between Duncan and herself? How could it? In just four days? After that last evening . . .

He was here, coming in at the far end of the corridor. Which meant he had come up three flights of stairs.

His purposeful strides brought him quickly to where she waited, searching his face for just one intimate sign. But the smile in her eyes was quickly subdued because he looked quite unapproachable as he went past her into Sister's inner office and she had to follow.

He stood, with one hand on the desk, facing her.

'I wanted to talk to you . . .' he said seriously.

'I came back last night . . .' she began tentatively.

His expression didn't change. 'I know . . .'

'You didn't phone,' she pressed.

'No. Would you have been there if I had?'

'My train was very late, but I was home just after nine.'

He broke in. 'I know what time your train got in. I came to meet you. In fact, I wasted three hours at that infernal station last night.'

'Then, why didn't I see you?'

He turned away to stare out of the window, his face unreadable, but it was his voice which caused the ache in her throat. 'Because you only had eyes for the man you were with, Meryl,' he ground out furiously, keeping his voice very low.

'Oh—Duncan . . .' her hand went out to touch the sleeve of his white coat. 'I hardly know him . . .'

'Well enough to go off in his car last night and for him to come here looking for you today.'

'He was here today on duty,' she told him quietly. 'It was quite by chance that I ran into him.'

'That isn't quite good enough, Meryl.'

She was aware only of the hurt and a feeling of resentment so she replied coolly, 'I'm afraid it will have to be for the moment, Dr Heyer. Did you want to discuss your patient?'

He seemed surprised by her change of tone. But because he was, after all, in charge of the new patient and had some observations he wanted to make, he proceeded to do so in his most authoritative manner before starting to walk away, leaving her bereft.

Before she could recover, the phone bleeped outside and, lifting it, she called his name.

'For you . . .' she said, handing it to him, not daring to meet his eyes in case he saw the brightness of a tear in hers. 'It's Casualty.'

Meryl didn't see him leave. The next moment she was trying to reassure a husband whose wife was on spinal traction and who had been waiting to catch her the moment she was free. But twenty minutes later he was again at the other end of the telephone.

'I'd like another patient admitted, Staff Nurse. You do have a bed? He's male . . .'

Her brain ran ahead of the fact that it was him. 'Now, Dr Heyer?'

'In half an hour, shall we say?'

'Yes. That will be possible.'

He must have heard the acceptance in her voice; knew that she would have to do some shuffling around and needed time, though few surgeons ever took that into consideration when demanding a bed for one of their patients.

And when she came out of one of the small wards where she had helped a nurse quickly prepare the bed just vacated, having moved that patient out on to the balcony, she drew in her breath quickly at the sight of him, calmly sitting in Sister's chair, turning over the pages of a patient's record notes, as if he had all the time in the world.

Going up to the table, she asked if he wanted this patient on traction also.

'Certainly. That's why I'm here. To see that it is exactly right.'

He wouldn't have dared say that to Sister Plumb, and he knew it. Meryl's eyes met his levelly. Even her junior staff nurse, about to take a sphygmomanometer from the huge white cupboard nearby, threw a surprised glance in their direction at the edge in his voice.

'This patient has been seen in Outpatients,' he began. 'He'll be on pelvic traction for the next few days—obviously the pain in his lower back has worsened which is why I've admitted him as an emergency, pending a laminectomy and possible fusion, to be decided when Mr Williams has had a look at him. Meanwhile . . . Ah—here he comes. Which room?'

'This one . . .' She indicated to the porters where to take the man, prone on the trolley, aware that Duncan was right behind her. Watching the transition from trolley to bed silently he then turned and walked away in the direction of the geriatric ward where the older women were recovering from his surgery. His hands were deep in his trouser pockets now, his eyes on the floor, which she recognised as one of his traits when he was thinking deeply. But he would be back when the necessary apparatus was in place to supervise the stringing up for himself. And it wasn't a bad thing because it usually took at least half an hour. And already the supper trolleys were being wheeled into the corridor.

Nurse Ralph was only too glad to escape when he returned and she was dismissed to help with the meals. Dr Heyer in this mood made her nervous.

The patient in the bed, although in great pain, was relieved to know that at last something definite was being done to help him, which made their task easier. And afterwards Duncan followed her back to the table, reminding her that he had prescribed pain killers for that night.

'It will probably seem the longest he has ever known,' he remarked cryptically.

But Meryl found nothing to say to him. She was puzzled and disappointed by his attitude towards her. But she was not at liberty even to think about her own problems until she climbed the stairs to her flat around eight-thirty that evening, breathing a sigh of relief when she found it empty, Jenny having gone out. After all, it was Saturday night. She couldn't have made small talk. She just needed to be quite alone, she told herself, as she switched on the electric fire.

But did she? Hadn't she longed for tonight, thinking that she and Duncan would be together again? Yet, today she had been met with a steely, disapproving expression on that face which had become so dear to her. Because he had been there to meet her off the train after all. But how could she know that? Why shouldn't she accept a lift from someone else? Surely he knew it hadn't meant anything more than that?

When the phone rang she had kicked off her shoes and

was staring unseeingly at the television screen, taking in absolutely nothing of what she saw. Simply using it as some form of escapism or even to unwind; her nerves were all coiled up inside her head.

Duncan said purposefully, brooking no argument, 'Meryl—I shall be waiting outside in just ten minutes. If you are not there, I shall presume it is because you don't want to be and I won't wait.'

'You know that isn't true,' she answered recklessly. But he had cut off.

Was it an ultimatum? Of course it was. Should she go? She must; if only to prove him wrong in his suppositions. In any case, there was no time to stand and stare frustratingly at the silent phone, although all kinds of adjectives flashed through her mind while she got out of uniform and pulled a green wool sweater dress over her head. Then, brushing her hair hard in front of the mirror, which helped, she regarded the rebellious green eyes with a rather unhappy, even uncertain gaze, before reaching for her favourite perfume spray, then adding another touch of lipstick to rosy lips.

Zipping her feet into brown suede leather boots, she pulled on her warm coat and, looking down, saw his car nosing into the space under a street lamp where she couldn't fail to see it. So, slinging her bag over one shoulder, she hastily switched off the room light to show that she was leaving, then, closing the door, ran lightly down the stairs and out into the forecourt, across the flagstones, to where he had already opened the car door for her.

Casting a surreptitious glance at his impassive expression, she slid into the seat beside him.

As the car moved forward he said in a rather strained voice, 'I'm glad you decided to come.'

Meryl didn't speak. So why had she? And for how

long did he intend to treat her like an errant schoolgirl? Suddenly, the ache in her throat became a strong challenge not to cry. So her head went up defiantly. 'Where are we going?'

He kept his eyes on the road. 'The one place we can be sure of some privacy,' he answered briefly.

'Your flat?'

He nodded. 'Of course. I think there are some points which need to be clarified. Don't you?'

'It depends on which points, as you call them, you are talking about,' she murmured a little throatily, while still trying to hang on to her hurt pride; sad at the loss of the rapport which had been between them.

There were no more pin pricks of contention between them, each was silent until the door of his flat closed behind them. Switching on the table lamps and fire brought a welcome glow to his room immediately. Meryl stood just inside the door and slipped her coat off. He took it, coming back to turn her round to face him, both hands biting into her shoulders while his eyes sternly searched her face until, with a muffled groan, his arms closed around her and he strained her to his hard, lean body, until it hurt.

'I can't lose you now,' he muttered raggedly, 'just when I was so sure I had found the one woman for me.' He stood back regarding her ruefully. 'Was I being premature, Meryl? Be completely honest with me, darling. But I have to know, before I get in any deeper.'

'You—are not giving me much chance to say anything,' she said softly, taking his hand and leading him over to the settee.

Now her lips had curved into their usual relaxed shape; a half smile quivered at the corners as she looked up into his waiting eyes. She knew now that everything was going to be all right. He loved her. He was jealous, that was all.

'Come and sit down.'

Throwing himself on to the settee, he said restlessly, 'We know very little about each other, which is why I have to explain what led up to this, I suppose.'

'You—don't have to.'

'I think I do. You see—you've become very special in my life now, Meryl, more than you know, and seeing you the other night,' his voice husked over, 'getting off that train with another man, was like a punch on the chin. I'm afraid I fumed a bit—apart from the disappointment when you disappeared together. I was convinced it was someone you knew—rather well.'

'Oh—Duncan . . .' she cried in mock exasperation. 'Why didn't you just show? Or even phone later?'

'I know. But there you were together again today. What on earth am I to conclude from that, Meryl? Are you going on seeing him?'

'Of course not,' she said, and now her eyes were jade green in the lamplight, filled with a tugging emotion which threatened tears, of relief, not pain. She managed a tentative smile, while her fingers slid beneath the hand on his knee. 'I only want to be with you; surely you knew that . . .'

'Oh—my darling . . .' His voice sounded unsteady as he reached for her, cradling her in his arms. 'You can't imagine what I've been feeling.'

'I think I can,' she murmured before his mouth closed over hers and there was nothing but the drowning, wanting of strong kisses, until her lips felt bruised and her senses were swimming. She had never experienced such arousal as her fingers moved in the thick, soft hair at the back of his head, needing to touch and hold him close to her.

Passion mounted fast and Duncan's strong features took on a new strength, welding them together in a bond of discovery and response to each other's questing need, so that when, with a mammoth effort, he drew away from her, dragging out a deep breath, holding her at arm's length, they both regarded each other's flushed faces a little ruefully while he muttered, 'I hate to let you go—do I have to, darling?'

'You know the answer to that,' she said, leaning to press her lips to his face, her own breathing still difficult to control. But her eyes were shining as her arms slipped around his neck and as he pulled her to her feet she knew beyond any shadow of doubt as he moulded her to his body that he was finding it desperately hard to let her go.

But, with a gigantic effort, he went to fetch her coat, coming back with it and his own determinedly, 'I . . .' he said firmly, 'am taking you back right now. But oh—my sweet—nothing will ever be the same again, will it? You do know that.'

'Of course . . .' She slid her arms into the coat he was holding, feeling his arms go round her, pulling her back against him before turning her round for a final kiss. It was more like a kiss full of promise and quite satisfying in itself. Together they left the warmth of his room and went out into the icy night. The first snow flakes had begun to fall, covering everything with a white sprinkling of beauty.

'Oh—how perfectly lovely everything looks, Duncan—those trees, positively ethereal—aren't they?'

'You . . .' he said grimly, 'are a romantic, of course. If this keeps up we are in for a hectic work load tomorrow, my lass . . .'

'Oh . . .' she breathed, her eyes like stars, 'no one has ever called me that before. I like it.'

Apart from flashing her an indulgent glance, he needed to concentrate on his driving for the rest of the short, hilly journey. When he drew up at the hospital gates, snow was forming in peaks on his windscreen and she urged him to get home quickly.

'Either that, or stay here tonight,' he muttered, looking upwards. 'It's going to be extremely hazardous by morning.'

'Just think . . .' she murmured dreamily, 'under all that snow there are snowdrops and primroses and wild violets, all waiting to come through. It's going to be spring before we know it. What a lovely thought, Duncan.'

He gave a small groan of resignation as his arm slid round her shoulders and he pulled her almost roughly close to the tweed of his jacket. 'Oh—I love you . . .' he muttered against the soft silkness of her hair. 'I wonder if you know how much?'

'There will be lots of time to find out . . .' she told him happily, as, kissing him quickly with her lips pressed to his strong face, she gently moved towards the door. 'Don't go back tonight. You have a bed here, don't you?'

'Oh, yes. No problem. I think I'd be wise to stay while I'm here. These hills can be unnegotiable once this snow really gets going.'

'Goodnight,' her smile stayed with him.

He watched her go inside, then drove around to the almost empty car park. He would have preferred to be going back to his own flat; the hospital environment had a way of brain-washing one, while in his own place he could have thought out a lot of future plans which he now decided to shelve for the moment. Only one had really been formulated. The most important—that he wanted to marry Meryl, have her for his wife, possess her utterly. Nothing else would do, but to know that she was his alone.

After that night, Meryl's whole working life changed too. Meeting Duncan along a corridor, or dealing with him on the wards, in Sister's absence, added impetus to her day and she couldn't always hide the glow of happiness from speculative eyes when they happened to meet unexpectedly. And because of the treacherous conditions outside the hospital, he was on the wards even more than usual. But usually she was in control of her emotions enough to avoid gossip erupting too seriously. Except that Jenny knew they were seeing each other at every available opportunity.

The snow did not last long and within two weeks the roads were clear again. The following Sunday they were both free for the whole day and Duncan called for her in the morning, driving them out into the country for a pub lunch.

Afterwards they walked to the top of a hill. Both were breathless from the climb when, without any warning, he turned her to face him. Behind her the downs, green after the snow revitalisation, rolled gently away to the river, sparkling in the spring sunshine. Her hair blew across her face and he lifted a hand to hold it back while he put into words the longing in his heart and asked her when she would marry him.

'Not if . . .' she asked laughingly, 'when?'

'But you knew that already,' his face was serious now. 'Darling—I love you—I want you. Of course we are going to be married. I've thought of nothing else. So yes—it's when?'

'Soon—if you're sure that is what you want.' Her words were lost as he pulled her close in a locked embrace. When they drew apart she gave a little cry of pleasure. 'Oh, look, Duncan . . .' Beneath their feet and close under the bushes of green shoots erupting from the bark, little clumps of pale yellow primroses were bursting through the crinkled brown leaves; near them, the first delicate purple heads and green leaves of the wood violets.

'They're very early, surely?' Duncan went to look more closely. 'Do you want to take a clump back with you?'

'Oh, no. Let them stay where they belong. But . . .' her fingers moved in his strong hand, 'I'll always think of today, here with you, when I see the first ones every spring.'

'Oh . . .' he said indulgently, his hand gripping hers as they began to walk back down to where they had left the car. 'I can't wait to show you my part of the world. I want you to meet my family. They'll never believe I've at last found a girl like you. So—when Meryl? Easter?'

'You mean, to get married? Well—let me get used to the idea first,' she begged, finding it impossible to keep the joy and excitement from her voice. Not that there was any reason why she should. It was unbelievable that she was going to be Duncan's wife. And only now were all the implications beginning to filter through. She would phone Elizabeth tonight—but she knew exactly what she would say. Dear practical Elizabeth. 'I'm so happy for you—but—you are absolutely sure about it, aren't you?'

Oh, yes. She was sure. She had never known it possible to love a man as she loved Duncan.

'A penny for your thoughts,' he asked as he unlocked the car, looking across the roof of it to where she stood dreamily waiting, while his eyes were reflecting his own deeper feelings too.

'I was thinking that I have just promised to spend the

rest of my life, hopefully, with one man and it's the most wonderful feeling.'

'You do say the loveliest things at the most inconvenient moments, my sweet,' he said, shaking his head, before sliding quickly into his seat and reaching out his hand to pull her in beside him. 'You are quite sure, then.'

'Quite. I know what I want too, you know,' she murmured before his lips stopped her.

When the car turned on to the road again she watched his strong profile and knew that he was very happy.

'You're looking very pleased with yourself, Dr Heyer,' she said teasingly.

'Why not? I've just become engaged.'

'Officially?'

'Oh—definitely,' he gave her a startled glance. 'Does that mean we have to make some sort of an announcement?'

'Not unless you want to,' she assured him happily. 'It really only concerns us, doesn't it?'

'But I'd like to buy you a ring.'

'And I would love to have one.'

Putting her hand impulsively on the knee of his beige cords, his own came to cover it firmly.

'Duncan—while I'm longing to shout it from the roof-tops and for everyone to know about us, couldn't we keep it to ourselves for just a little while; until we do have a definite date and all the arrangements have been made?'

'If that is what you want,' he said thoughtfully. 'And, of course, you must come with me to Scotland to meet my parents, or even half way. But soon, I think. Yes—I see you mean—there are a number of things to be considered aren't there? A honeymoon for one. I believe my holiday period is the first three weeks of June. It seems rather a long way off.'

'Oh—no—it isn't really.' She reached for the diary in her handbag. 'June 1st—is on a Friday.'

'Better make it the 2nd then.'

A quiver ran down her spine and into her toes. She said breathlessly, 'That's barely four months away.'

'So?' He flashed her a meaningful smile. 'I wish it was tomorrow—or even sooner. Why don't we drive back now, change and go out for dinner tonight? Surely a celebration is indicated.'

'What a lovely idea.'

That evening they sat facing each other across a table in the exclusive restaurant to which he had brought her, where the management understood how much the lighting and decor really mattered, providing the privacy of alcoves and soft, if piped, music and excellent menus and service. Meryl had never felt so pampered and Duncan was at his most caring, rising to the occasion by ordering champagne and a superb meal.

She really felt they belonged together now; life would be everything she was in tune with. She could look forward to being his wife with every confidence. It was like a dream coming true. Never—would she be a girl on her own, ever again.

He raised his glass. 'To us, my darling,' he said simply, and echoing his words she lifted her glass too.

CHAPTER FIVE

BECAUSE Meryl had insisted that something should be decided about their wedding plans before he went off to London for his seminar, on a particular evening they were sitting making notes together in Duncan's flat. It was quiet; the kind of tranquillity she liked after a hectic day.

But now she looked up at the note of impatience in his voice as he studied his diary. 'This . . .' he asserted, 'is becoming even more complicated. Why on earth can't we just take off and do it? Tell them all afterwards.'

'Oh—you know we can't. Your parents would be so hurt if we did that.'

'And your stepmother . . .'

'She hates to be called that, Duncan. She is Elizabeth.'

'Elizabeth, then. Do you have any more relatives who simply have to be invited?'

Meryl wisely ignored his tone.

'I would love my Aunt and Uncle Lewis to be there,' she said thoughtfully, 'but he isn't well enough to travel.'

'So—apart from Elizabeth—there are only friends—yours and mine. So—why don't we get married in Scotland?' he concluded, putting his diary away in his pocket.

'Oh—I don't know . . .' he heard the uncertainty in her voice and made an instant decision.

'Meryl—I'm taking you home with me as soon as you can have a few days off. We'll do it in one day if you're willing, or make a stop-over. That way you can meet my family and we can make some final plans for June.'

She agreed at once. 'It sounds wonderful,' she said happily, 'but I can't just demand leave like that. I will see what can be arranged though. And what about your schedule?'

'There is the Easter break coming up—I think I could be off then.'

She sighed. 'I wish we could just find a little church in the country and get married,' she said wistfully.

'Why don't we, then?'

'Oh—because we don't want to start that way. Rushed and upsetting everyone—and there is your seminar and Sister away for two weeks at the end of March, and I wanted to finish my course before I gave all my attention to you and being a wife and . . .'

Colour flooded her face at the intentness of his gaze. He was still able to do that. Command her in this way, because of their different status at the hospital. For too many months she had been conscious of the fact that he could, with just one look, mesmerise her, with a resultant tingling up and down her spine.

'It's all important to me,' she finished lamely.

He gathered her close, almost roughly. 'Nothing,' he said huskily, 'is more important than our future, being together. Yet it seems we are letting us—that—take second place.'

'You know that isn't true,' she said softly, lifting her arms around his neck to meet behind his head. 'We're together now—aren't we? And it isn't long before . . .'

'Don't be so practical,' he muttered, drawing her closer to his masculine body so that she was fully aware of every part of him. 'Darling—I want you, all of you. Why in God's name do we have to make all these ridiculous plans? Why wait?'

She was asking herself the same question as his lips found hers, burning in their passionate searching, and she lost the will even to try to think logically any more, drowning in the sensations his nearness evoked, content then to leave it all to his abject need. But it was he who put her away from him at last with a soft groan and, because her legs were weak and trembling, she sank down on to the settee and covered her face with her hands which shook slightly. Duncan pulled her to her feet, running a finger down the flushed cheek as he took her hands away, smoothing away a tear which she hadn't known was there.

'Is it possible?' he asked softly, looking deep into the green depths of her eyes raised to his, 'that, when we make love, completely, it will be the first time for you—that I shall be the only one ever to . . .'

Her murmured, 'Yes . . .' made him close his eyes momentarily before he hugged her again, but this time with returning control, before he said firmly,

'Then—my darling girl—I am going to have to wait until you are my wife to possess you utterly; and that's a promise. I do have a streak of idealism it seems, under this androcentric hide of mine.' He lifted her chin, kissing her nose gently. 'It is what you want too—isn't it?'

Meryl nodded, pressing her face to his now, their understanding complete.

Next day, Duncan phoned his parents, imparting his news, which delighted them, and promising that he would be bringing Meryl to meet them in April. If she couldn't take enough time to make the journey they all agreed to meet in London. Elizabeth, too, received a phone call, putting her in the picture and sharing Meryl's happiness too.

'I can't wait to meet him,' she said, when she knew the

wedding would be in June. 'I shall start looking at hats right away. And where are you going for a honeymoon?'

'Oh—we haven't got that far yet,' Meryl told her excitedly. And somehow—it didn't matter too much. They would be together—that was what mattered.

If other members of staff at the hospital suspected that Dr Heyer and Staff Nurse Summers were having a serious affair, not a word reached their ears. But it would have been impossible not to notice the new lightness in his step, especially on the corridors of D-Level, or miss the light of happiness in Meryl's eyes these days, nor how easily the smile seemed to bubble over at the least provocation. She was in love, and it showed.

Sister Plumb kept an observant eye on both of them, but she couldn't be sure yet, so she decided to wait until she was. She didn't want to lose her senior staff nurse and her own holiday was close. She was looking forward to a well-earned break and the coach trip to Austria with another member of the nursing staff.

'It's been a lethal three months since Christmas,' she told Meryl on her last day. 'I feel really jaded.'

Meryl agreed. The work load had been very heavy. And would be, even more so, for the next two weeks. But after that—her spirits soared and imagination took off. Why—she could be going to Scotland for her own spring holiday with the man she loved. No prying eyes— just each other. What bliss . . . Like a dream.

Sister left her fully staffed, which was something. There were other sisters-in-charge on call if she needed them. But she had coped before and always accepted her new responsibility as a challenge.

It was during the late afternoon on the first day of Sister's absence when Jeremy Banks, the young house doctor on duty, finished writing up a patient's notes at the long table outside the wards where they all gathered for instructions and the endless writing of histories. He stood up, giving Meryl a tentative grin as she joined him.

She smiled back at him, because she always felt a little sorry for the housemen, either male or female. Generally regarded as being terribly overworked; from their own personal view it was probably the worst year of their training lives. Newly qualified, but lacking the practical knowledge and approach of the more experienced surgeons and doctors, every single day was fraught with keeping face, absorbing everything which came their way, learning from their mistakes and getting to know every patient whose history they were taking at that particular moment because their senior had to know about it too.

Now Dr Jeremy Banks straightened his back and looked hesitatingly into the green glint of her eyes.

'Something wrong?' she asked lightly as she took the folder from him. He carefully put his pen away in the pocket of his white coat before asking quickly,

'I—was wondering if you'd come out with me this evening?'

'I'm so sorry—I . . .'

'Do you have a boy friend? Oh—of course—you do . . .'

'Yes . . .' she answered softly.

'Thought you might. Still—there's no harm in asking—you didn't mind?'

'Not at all.' Her smile was soft because she sensed his discomfiture and it worked, because his face relaxed and he gave her an answering smile as he leaned over her shoulder to point out something he had written. 'I want to have a word with Dr Heyer about that. It could be relevant.'

Duncan had, unnoticed, come from one of the consulting rooms and something about the gentle way they smiled at each other, seemed to have quite the opposite effect upon him as he came purposefully towards the table, positively glaring at them both, addressing Jeremy.

'Are you through here, Dr Banks?' he began without preamble.

'Yes. I . . .'

'Then I suggest you catch up on those reports I'm waiting for and not waste time here.'

It was an awkward moment by any standards, as the young doctor flashed him a glance which clearly said, 'What did I do?' but he immediately walked away down the corridor. Duncan led the way into the inner office and Meryl followed close behind, feeling her hackles rising.

'Duncan—what on earth,' she began, when he turned to face her.

'You should know better than to encourage a first-year man on the wards,' he said angrily. 'Do you know what that looked like? Grinning at each other like two Cheshire cats out there . . .'

'We were discussing Mr Thorn's notes, which he had just finished,' she said icily. 'A breathing space and nothing more.' Her eyes clouded over. 'How could you speak to him like that—and in front of me?' she asked worriedly.

'Okay. I'm sorry.'

'Apologise to him, not me. It's so unlike you. Is anything wrong?'

'I don't know. You tell me. You were rather close together from where I was standing. Is that necessary? And shouldn't you be setting some kind of an example to your pupil nurses who don't need any encouragement to do the same?'

Before she could think of an appropriate answer the red light began flashing above her head.

'Excuse me . . .' she turned, leaving him standing there looking after her disappearing print dress, and the white cap, looking very precarious on the specially uplifted head. He didn't know that she was biting her lower lip as she hurried down the corridor, nor that the sun had gone out of the day for her. But all other thoughts left her when she saw that an elderly patient was apparently choking on a piece of orange and already looking blue.

'Go and fetch Dr Heyer,' she directed the junior nurse who had pressed the bell. 'He was in the office. Hurry . . .' In the few seconds before he arrived, she had managed to dislodge the blockage but was still thankful for his quick response. And he didn't leave until the scared patient was sufficiently recovered.

'She'll do now,' he said to Meryl, as she drew back the curtains around the bed. 'Perhaps Nurse can watch her for a while.' Which meant that he wanted Meryl to leave with him.

In the corridor they discussed the patient who had angina, but Meryl found it hard to look at him. She was still smarting from his attack on the houseman and herself.

'Tonight?' he asked quietly. 'You will still come?'

'Of course.'

His eyes moved over her lovely shining hair. 'I shall be through by eight-thirty and I'll wait for you by the gate.'

She nodded, only now meeting his eyes briefly before he turned and walked away down the corridor, heavily for him. It was so unlike him to speak down to a junior doctor that way. They had to talk this thing out, she resolved. For it was as if a little demon lurked ready to pounce if he even saw her talking to another man. Would this jealousy persist even after they were married? she wondered uneasily.

She took a very deep breath, shrugging it off for the present, because there were a dozen other immediate problems requiring answers and she had been trained to cope with them one by one and switch off to another, probably quite different one—only sometimes, they seemed to come in batches.

Quickly walking along to the dining-room half an hour later, she saw Jeremy come from the doctor's dining-room and spoke to him. 'I'm terribly sorry about—all that . . .' she said quietly.

He shrugged. 'Came out of the blue rather, didn't it? But it's okay. Dr Heyer buzzed me just now. Caught him at rather a bad moment, it seems.' He shrugged philosophically, giving her a rueful smile. 'I think I'm almost broken in,' he said, 'and as for Dr Heyer, I've got a lot to be grateful for—he's been marvellous all through the year. So forget it. I must fly—got to do some tests and get them hurried through by seven tonight.'

Well, she thought passively as she sipped her tea, that was the houseman's lot. Always in demand, working unlimited hours, every day, absorbing more knowledge—expected to take part in theatre, in front of experienced eyes, sweating blood themselves; hands shaking, sick with nerves, the first time. Every other doctor had gone through it during his own first fledgling year; made the same mistakes and emerged, those who made it, to become qualified life-savers in every hospital in the world.

She jumped up as Jenny and another nurse came to her table with their tea, exchanging greetings. 'Don't go . . .'

'I have to rush,' she told them in explanation. 'It's

becoming rather a fraught day and I will be very relieved when it's over . . .'

'We're having one too,' Jenny affirmed. 'Well—it's Monday, isn't it?'

Back on the ward she saw that Dr Gree, Mr Williams's house doctor, was talking to one of his patients and making notes. Young and attractive, she delighted the top surgeon with her cool courage and intellect. But while she was thorough, she didn't spend as long taking patients' histories as Jeremy. Meryl wished Duncan had seen him sitting patiently listening to Mrs Thorn's aches and pains, trying to sort out the relevant ones from the less vital symptoms, while his pen travelled over the pages, asking question after question and writing the answers.

Jenny was also going out that evening. Meryl, waiting to use the bathroom, was filling in by running the cleaner over the faded carpet in the lounge and a quick duster along the bookshelves and the top of the television set. She wished, as she left the kitchen neat and clean, for the hundredth time, that her flatmate would make life a little easier by keeping everything in its rightful place. Now that she was spending more evenings with Duncan, there was less time for necessary chores and everything was just scrambled through, which was not her way at all.

But—she told herself brightly, as she waited—not for too much longer now. Soon she would be living in Duncan's flat. They had reached a decision about this because he was not sure what his future plans were at this stage.

'We will have a house of our own, of course, in time,' he had promised firmly. 'A real home.'

'So—you don't really want to stay here in the South?'

'It depends on a number of things but, just now, I'd

prefer not to make fast decisions. You don't mind, darling?'

'Of course not. I love the flat anyway.'

'Well—we can make a few improvements if you like. Such as a new bed—for one thing,' he said teasingly.

'Getting married wasn't part of your plans, was it?'

'Not until you,' he whispered tenderly, 'and then it was very much on my mind. Now—I can't wait. I want you to be my wife, more than anything else. Then perhaps I can implement other plans which are in embryo at present. Something we can perhaps do together. I can't say more just yet.'

'Sounds exciting.'

Now she stood musing over his words. Stretching her arms above her head; oh, what a wonderful life they would have together.

Jenny came dashing in then, pulling on her coat. 'The bathroom's all yours. I'm off now.'

'Well, thanks,' Meryl said drily. 'I've got just fifteen minutes.'

'Oh—he'll wait. You've really got him hooked, haven't you?' she said mischievously. 'Lucky you—but he isn't my type. Now—if it was Dr Jerram you could have competition. Oh—boy . . .'

Meryl ignored her banter as she went to get ready. Besides, tonight she was missing the usual glow in the eyes looking thoughtfully back at her from the bathroom mirror. There was something muted behind the grey-green pupils, also an awareness of some complexity in her mind which she couldn't or didn't want to categorise. But the thought struggled to be recognised. How well did she know the man she was going to marry? It was natural, that having accepted that they were in love, there were new things to discover all the time. But this inate jealousy which seemed to rear its head every time he saw her just talking to another man; that was something else. What could she do about it? Only constantly reassure him that he was the one man in her life who meant anything. But she shouldn't have to do that. Not now.

Usually she rushed out to meet him, glowing with that kind of happiness which only came when they were together but, tonight, beneath her smile, was an ache of apprehension which only he could eradicate. She must go. His car was there now, parked under the street lamp.

Slipping in beside him, his hand reaching to close over hers already, all doubts fled. She felt only tender understanding. His problems were hers, although, as yet, he hadn't admitted to his jealousy being a problem—perhaps he never would. But she knew that it was and she must help him to overcome it, whether he was aware of it or not, before it became a stumbling block and could ruin everything for both of them. But after she had tentatively brought it up and they had talked out the day's incident in the warmth of the flat, it began to lose its importance in the overriding fusion of mounting passion, hard to resist, which blurred his voice as he promised that once she belonged to him there would be no fear of losing her.

'So—it's possession,' she said softly, not waiting for his answer because her own aching need was overtaking all other thinking; then—'Oh—Duncan—I want to belong to you—I do—now; I want you to love me, tonight . . .'

'No—no . . .' he said huskily, resisting her arms and the kisses which had brought desire to an almost impossible limit. 'I'm conservative enough to want to make love to you on our wedding night. It's what you really want too, isn't it, sweetheart?'

'Yes—yes it is.' She recovered quickly. 'Can I make us some coffee—hot and strong?'

'Please.' He leaned back, watching her, imagining her in his home soon, knowing the period of readjustment was going to be a completely new experience because he had been used to living on his own since leaving the university. He needed time to adjust to other things as well. Which reminded him that he should have caught up with his notes for the seminar next week.

'You'll enjoy that,' Meryl said as she joined him and he mentioned the work he still had to do in preparation. 'Meeting other medics and exchanging views must be an exciting experience.'

'It's an exhausting week usually,' he told her. 'So much material gets packed into those few days that one emerges feeling punch drunk at the end of it. One needs time to sort out the wheat from the chaff.'

'I haven't heard that expression in ages,' she remarked as she finished her coffee. 'But Duncan—could we go soon. I'm on early duty tomorrow and I feel all in tonight. With Sister away—it's a bit wearing.'

'We're both burning the candle at both ends, my sweet,' he said, encountering her eyes' meaning fully.

'Yes, well, it shows,' she told him ruefully, as he slipped her coat over her shoulders, then went to turn off the lights.

'So this is really our last time together,' she mused when he outlined his plans until he left, because of their varying duty hours and his evening lectures.

'Yes—I suppose so. I shall be back on Friday evening, I hope—and we'll go out for dinner on Saturday.

'Fine. I'll look forward to that. Oh—it's Jenny's birthday on Friday and she is planning some kind of party.'

'I see. Who will be there?'

'I've no idea. As many as she can get inside the door, if

I know her. She's probably inviting the whole of the hospital staff,' she finished laughingly. 'If you're back in time, why don't you come too?'

'Heaven forbid,' he said fervently. 'I shall be looking forward to Saturday. I'll call you, of course.'

Once before he left they had been alone in her office and he had quickly squeezed her arm because other nurses were within earshot just outside.

'I love you . . .' he said softly.

'And I you.' The warmth of her smile was enough to make him leave her with a light step, although his face was inscrutable; hers too, as she watched his white coat disappear around the bend in the corridor.

She missed him during the ensuing time that he was away, but he phoned twice, bringing a glow of warmth across the wires to sustain her. Besides, there were a lot of preparations to make for Jenny's party. It seemed that to avoid any complaints from the others in the block, she had extended them an open invitation too.

The party opened on a hilarious note because the first arrivals, two male nurses, had already started celebrating, dumping their bottles of wine on the table along with those provided by Jenny and Meryl. It already looked like the bar of a club.

By nine-thirty the party was in full swing as people came and went. Most of the nurses were about ready for a real let-your-hair-down rave-up and Meryl got lost, eventually giving up trying to keep some semblance of order as the wine and beer circulated. Several of the trainee doctors came too. Jenny insisted that she hadn't invited them, but Meryl was sceptical about that and could only hope that they wouldn't drag it out once the food was gone. She was kept too busy to really enjoy the party herself because Jenny was already threatening to do a strip-tease act, except that she could barely stand up. And while Jenny was off duty next day, she was not.

But gradually they began to drift away; some actually going on to yet another party, and by eleven-thirty the flat was suddenly quiet and empty. Jenny had been helped into bed by two other nurses, resisting offers of assistance from the male guests who were only too willing to lend a hand. And this was when Meryl's great diplomacy reminded them that others in the block were probably trying to sleep, they took the hint and began a steady exodus, until she was left to survey a room full of glasses and empty plates and the usual debris.

But she attacked it all while her bath water was running, knowing that it would help her unwind and sleep better.

When she went into the bathroom the warm foamy water looked so inviting she slipped out of her clothes right then and, stretching her arms above her head, gently relaxed the tired muscles of her arms and shoulders before stepping into the bath. Oh—goodness—I'm tired, she thought; desperately so—but tomorrow Duncan and she would be together again. He obviously hadn't got back in time to come to the party, or decided against it—for which she couldn't blame him. But when he had phoned two nights ago he had said he would be calling for her at seven-thirty on Saturday. 'Dinner is at eight. I've booked a table for us, darling. Can't wait to see you. It seems a lifetime.'

She had laughed, deliciously smug, because he had missed her too. Now she was counting the hours to what promised to be a romantic evening with the man she loved so very much.

She was drying herself on the large white bath towel when she thought she heard the doorbell tinkle softly. It must be one of the nurses. She had found a handbag behind a chair. Perhaps she had just missed it. Padding across to the door she opened it, keeping the chain still in place. Duncan stood there quizzically, even teasingly, looking into her flushed face.

'It's you,' she cried joyfully, sliding back the chain and letting him in, while she struggled to hold the bath towel in place.

'The party seems to be over,' he said softly. 'I saw the light on as I came from the hospital. They had a scare on and called me in, knowing that I was back. I couldn't resist coming up. Oh—you're ready for bed. Sorry, darling.'

'It doesn't matter. I'm so glad you did, although I'm . . .'

'Yes . . .' he grinned. 'I can see that.'

Her arm reached up around his neck.

'I—didn't expect you,' she began, waiting for the familiar strength of his arms around her. Instead, her arms were gripped, vice-like, bruising, as he pushed her away from him. She struggled to keep the towel from falling, puzzled by his narrowed eyes, the change to disgust, as they flashed past her. His lip curled.

'That is quite apparent,' he ground out. 'I can see that I wasn't expected. So—it was that kind of party, was it? Well—this time—you don't confuse my thinking, Meryl. I can see for myself.'

She turned her head, stung by his disparaging tone, his awful words, to see one of the new housemen, whom she didn't even remember, coming from her bedroom. He must have been in there asleep all the time. He still looked slightly drunk, bemusedly thinking that the party was still on, even a joke; until he recognised Dr Heyer standing there and glaring at him acidly.

'Oh—no . . .' her cry of protest came from her heart as she saw anger and recoil masking Duncan's features

as he jumped to an obvious conclusion. Only then did
Meryl realise the implication. He really thought she had
come from there too. That she . . . 'Oh—Duncan . . .'
she groaned, but no real sound came out. He had gone
anyway, leaving the door open. The cold night air came
in. She shivered from shock and from sheer exhaustion.

'Get out!' she ordered angrily as the young doctor
began to protest, explaining,

'Sorry—I've had four hours' sleep in two nights.
Sorry, I must have . . .'

'Just—get out!' Her voice was unrecognisable, no
longer the caring one everyone knew. She was very
angry, closing the door after him, desperate to be
alone.

It hadn't happened, it couldn't. How could Duncan
have jumped to those wrong conclusions? He hadn't
given her a chance to explain even. Stunned, and desperately tired, she went at last into her bedroom. The junior
doctor's head indentation still marked her pillow. He
had simply thrown himself down on top of her duvet,
dislodging it every time he turned over. Exhaustion and
a few drinks had driven him through the first open door
to oblivion. That she could understand—but not Duncan's immediate acceptance of her own guilt.

She lay, heavy with disappointment, frustration and a
desperate need to put it all right. But she knew in her
heart, even then, that nothing could replace his lack of
trust in her She felt physically sick and only dozed after
she had got up on two occasions.

In the morning her own anger was directed at Duncan
for daring to think she could have been capable of that
kind of subterfuge. She dragged herself wearily out of
bed, dashing cold water over her face, appalled when
she saw herself in the mirror. How on earth was she
going to take charge of wards full of patients feeling like

this? She could report sick, but after last night's party—no—she could not do that.

And Jenny, appearing in the doorway, did nothing to improve anything.

'I can't believe it! I didn't hear a thing. But Meryl, he couldn't have believed such a thing. Doesn't he know you better than that? I'm appalled . . .'

'So am I; and apparently, he doesn't,' Meryl said, handing her a glass of bismuth for her hangover, wondering how on earth she was going to get through the day. She had never, since losing her father, felt this utter sense of loss and deprivation. Duncan had held her heart in his hands. Now there was just no time to cry at the crack in it. For that was what it felt like.

CHAPTER SIX

IT seemed that everything conspired against her progress next day and, afterwards, she wondered how she had ever got through the morning with its accompanying problems and never ending 'Staff—what shall I do about Mr—— or Mrs——?' or 'Staff—can you come?' until the words rang in her ears and she had to resort to aspirin for the headache which throbbed relentlessly across her forehead. But nothing could erase the pain which had come with Duncan's derisive words last night; his readiness to believe that what he saw was some kind of sexual frolic between her and that exhausted young doctor who, after a few beers, had escaped to the nearest bed and slept. Her bed; and Duncan must have seen it in disarray; and her own damp tousled hair; her flushed cheeks; and known she was naked beneath the bath towel. And he had, without waiting, or thinking any further, turned away in disgust and chagrin, his face reflecting both.

Oh why hadn't he waited to hear the truth? That she hadn't even been to bed yet. Nor had she gone into her room since early evening. It could have been explained then; but not now. It was too late. Already he believed the worst.

At six, the relief Sister came to check that all was running smoothly but, seeing her pallor and that she was desperately tired, insisted on relieving her at once.

'You're not sickening for flu, are you? There's an awful lot of it about right now,' she commented, looking hard at Meryl as if she couldn't quite make up her mind.

But the wan staff nurse shook her head. 'I don't think so—but I do feel a bit under par. Perhaps an early night . . .'

Jenny was out and the flat was an oasis of quiet. She drew the curtains against the chill of the night outside and gave herself up to her own thoughts and misery.

All day she had dreaded meeting Duncan because it might have been too difficult to keep up the pretence and protocol expected and set a whisper circulating. Yet she had hoped for just one word which might have brought a chance to explain. Now there seemed no solution to this new impasse between them. Words like arrow thrusts were remembered again, arousing anger towards him as inate pride came to rescue her from the self-inflicted pain swirling around in her mind. She couldn't forgive him for the havoc he had done to their loving relationship; all that promise of a perfect life they were planning. They would have been together tonight, making even more plans and recapturing the warmth of their love after that long week of separation.

Closing her eyes against even that disappointment, she gave in to the pain of it all, letting it riot through her body until her hands covered her face and she sobbed brokenly. Because now there was an awful void of emptiness where there had been joy and so much still to come. No future with the man she really loved. All swept away like a giant wave demolishing a sand castle. 'Oh—Duncan . . .' she groaned. 'I would have trusted you first before anything.' But not he. His trust was a weak, fragile thing. His jealousy had won this time. And she had thought to combat it. But why did it blind him to any alternative? Why did he rush straight in with his first wrong impressions every time? Why had he allowed his possessiveness to blind him? Now—the face she had touched so lovingly, kissed with all of her newly-recognised passion, was that of a stranger and there would be no more intimate moments between them. No more searching kisses—no more touching—their relationship destroyed in embryo. Never would they know the joy of possession, of belonging—of tumultuous passion and loving.

But she still had her dignity. Her marvellous strength, and that she would not allow him to destroy. By next day she had reached her decision. It had come late at night as she wondered just how she was going to get through the coming months, seeing Duncan every day, talking with him, trying to hide her true feelings so that he didn't suspect the havoc he had caused. Now—her head was thrown back resolutely. She would leave this hospital and start again somewhere else. Perhaps in the West Country. It was a devastating decision but, once made, she would carry it through.

On Sunday, although Duncan was on call, he didn't show all day. Heavy-eyed from emotion and an almost sleepless night, Meryl managed to cope somehow, with the knowledge that Sister Plumb would be back tomorrow and then she would be able to relax her arduous responsibility and start to put her plans into action. She refused to allow Duncan to destroy her; and because of her sensitive, caring nature, this he could very easily do. Her pain could be absorbed, especially as it must be her own, and couldn't be shared with anyone else.

Sister's first words to her when she marched on to Orthopaedic next morning, infused with the invigorating air and benefits of her Austrian holiday, were, 'Good heavens, girl—what on earth have they done to you while I've been away? You've lost weight and you look dreadful. Are you okay?'

Meryl shrugged off her remarks, but not easily, going straight into the procedure of handing over to her senior with enormous relief. But she left it until later in the morning, when Sister was immersed once more into routine and the nurses were carrying out their tasks and everything apparently running smoothly, before she told her about her decision to leave.

'Have you actually given in your notice?' Sister Plumb wanted to know. 'Because if not—I suggest you think it over a little more. I don't know the reason, and you obviously aren't going to tell me—not the basic reasons for your decision—but don't do anything hasty, Staff. I'd hate to lose you—if it can be avoided.'

Wearily she said, 'I'm sorry. But I do have an appointment to see the Nursing Officer at twelve. That's why I had to tell you first.'

'Then, tell me . . .' Sister's eyes searched hers. 'Is it work—or is it personal?'

'Personal, actually. I—want to make a change—of hospital—everything.'

'I see. And—I can't help?'

'No. But thank you—just the same.'

Sister sighed in acceptance. 'Well, I'm truly sorry to lose you and so will everyone else be, but . . .'

The conversation came to an abrupt conclusion with the arrival of Mr Williams and his retinue, today comprising students too. She went to meet them and the whole wards became crowded with white coats and sheaves of notes and buzzing voices. Meryl escaped soon afterwards and made her way towards the Nursing Officer's rooms where her interview went along the same lines. But she was adamant. Her decision to leave the hospital had been made after a great deal of thought and was irrevocable. So there was no alternative. It was accepted, as she was firmly told, with the greatest reluctance.

When she came back along the corridor, Duncan was

leaving the accident ward. His firm, purposeful steps came to an abrupt halt when he saw her. The first leap of her heart sent the colour rushing to her face. Should she tell him?

But after that first hesitation he gave her the briefest of glances and continued to walk on by. His arrogance was impossible to take. Tears welled up behind her eyes; her throat ached as if it would close completely as she went slowly towards the lift. How could he do that to her? Now she hated him and, furiously angry, rushed into an empty lift so that she could dash away the tears he had caused and attempt to recover some semblance of control before she stepped out among people again.

And they were there—in the waiting lounge—relatives, visitors, doctors talking to them or each other, a receptionist, all noticing the uniformed figure with her head held high, but not one of them suspecting what turmoil was going on underneath that blue dress.

There were other contacts, of course. There had to be. The patients were an issue which couldn't be avoided. Sometimes he brought his houseman with him, or a student or two; sometimes Sister Plumb took care of him. But there were times when Meryl had to talk with him and this she did by meeting his eyes coolly, if he forced it, as he had that day, across a bed, when he asked a direct question. She had faced him with no embarrassment and it was he who had looked away first.

It was not a victory, for either of them. And afterwards, the aching sadness of it all had struck again. There was no consolation anywhere. Not even in the fact that if he found it that easy to erase the last weeks as if they had never been, it was just as well they had broken in time. For his love was obviously not as indestructible as hers and it wouldn't have stood the test of time in the kind of marriage any consultant doctor must have. She could only guess at those strains, but there had to be some. Or—her spirits lifted suddenly—could he just have been putting up a front? Should she tell him that she was leaving and give him time to assess that fact before it was too late? Because of the very special kind of love they had found together—shouldn't she try to break through and tell him what really happened? Her pride forbade it. She just could not bring herself to do that. Beg for his understanding of a situation which was bizzare to say the least. His sheer arrogance as he resumed his surgeon's image, using that as his escape line, only made her even more resentful, more determined that he should never know what he was doing to her.

She wasn't eating. Food had lost its flavour. She knew, by the span of her belt, that her waist was smaller. But the month was creeping by and she could only wait for the last day. But, waking with a sore throat and throbbing head one morning, was all she needed to complete her apathy. By midday her aching limbs confirmed her own diagnosis. She had to crawl back to bed.

Because it was not generally known until then that she was leaving, it didn't reach Duncan's ears until he missed her on the wards and had to deal with a strange staff nurse in charge during Sister's absence at a meeting.

He deliberately returned on the pretext of looking at a patient again, but when he was certain Sister Plumb would have returned, asking as he left,

'What has happened to Staff Nurse Summers?'

'She's on sick leave, Dr Heyer. Flu actually, but she hasn't been at all well lately. I've been quite worried about her.'

He made no comment, but Sister noticed a tightening of his lips and something in the momentary unguarded look he gave her set her thinking. He was concerned.

And he didn't know about her being ill either. So they weren't still seeing each other.

That evening she decided to take Meryl some flowers and check for herself what progress she was making. She was up, but so unlike her usual glowing self that Sister Plumb put her quickly back into her armchair again, wrapping the blanket firmly around her.

'Should you be out of bed?'

'Dr Graves said I might—just to get the feel of my legs back again.' She smiled weakly, the soft white house-coat making her dark hair and green eyes a strong contrast. 'I have to make some effort,' she went on, 'and my temp is down now.'

'Dr Heyer was asking about you today,' Sister said complacently.

'Oh . . .' There was an immediate reaction as the colour rushed to Meryl's face, which had, until then, been almost as white as her housecoat.

'He didn't know you had been ill,' Sister went on. 'He was very concerned.'

Meryl couldn't stop the trembling of her mouth. 'Really?' was all she could manage before the bright tears overflowed and she reached hurriedly for a tissue. 'This wretched flu,' she burst out, 'it—makes one feel terribly low . . .'

'You won't be coming back, you know,' Sister went on quietly. 'There is no way you are going to feel strong enough by the end of the week when your notice expires.'

'I know. I'm so sorry . . .'

'So—what will you do?'

'My stepmother phoned this morning and insists on driving up to take me back with her. Once I'm fit again I'll look for another job.' She smiled wanly. 'I'm afraid I haven't got that far yet.'

'Very wise of her. You'd never make the train journey.' She picked up her bag, ready to leave. 'Just relax and get your strength back, Meryl. I'll see you again before you go. Have you got some food in the flat?'

'Oh, yes. Jenny sees to that. She's been marvellous actually. Thanks for coming.'

But after Sister had gone she curled up in the big armchair, resting her head on her hand, despondently thinking about the future she had not envisaged as yet, because she would miss the hospital which had formed her background over the past four years so very much. But it was the only way she could even begin to get Duncan out of her life. The truth was, she didn't want to start trying to erase him. She could only long for the lost magic they had found together. Yet—she must do something.

The following afternoon, she had just come from the kitchen after making herself some tea, sinking gratefully into her chair and wearing her housecoat still, having made up her mind that she must dress tomorrow and pull herself together, when the door bell rang.

She had reached the stage when any visitor would be welcome. Switching on the lamp beside her, flooding the room in a soft glow, she got up to answer it. If only she didn't feel so lethargic—even her legs seemed to be hollow, so her progress was necessarily slow. But whoever was there had waited. She saw his shadow on the glass and remembered that Dr Graves had said he might look in. But she was shocked to see Duncan standing there, looking rather impatient, as if he wasn't very happy about coming at all.

'Can I come in?'

She stood back, feeling only weakness travelling over her body and it was he who closed the door, ordering her to go and sit down, while he slowly followed until she was curled back under her blanket again.

'I'm sorry you've been ill,' he began, 'but that's not why I'm here . . .'

'Won't you sit down?'

'No—I don't think so. I came because I heard today that you are leaving here. Is that true?' His voice sounded harsh, making her look up at him.

'Yes. This next week actually.' Even her voice had an apathetic ring while she fought to keep it from quivering with deeply unshed tears. If only then he had shown her his true feelings. Everything might have changed. Instead, he crossed to the window and looked down on to the cars passing either in or out of the hospital precincts, so that she couldn't see his face. Only his back; his reddish brown hair in the lamplight; his whole person making her ache unbearably while she waited for what he would say next.

'Well . . .' he averred, 'you have, I think, made the right decision. It has created an impossible situation where we are both having to meet constantly during working hours. In fact, I had even considered looking elsewhere myself.'

His words shocked her into saying chokingly, 'I feel— as if I don't know you at all. Yet—we were going to be married. Oh—please—just go away. I wish you hadn't come. We have absolutely nothing more to say to each other. I . . .' She pressed her hand to her trembling mouth. 'I can't believe this is happening . . .'

'But it has. I couldn't have believed what happened that night either—if I hadn't seen you both with my own eyes.' He turned back into the room, staring down at her with every muscle in his face taut with tension.

'You still believe that?'

'I saw you, Meryl,' he broke in, his voice grating on his words. 'My God—do you think I enjoyed seeing my future wife, like that, and that houseman leering at you from the door of your bedroom. Was that before or after your lovemaking? And—to think that I might never have known if I hadn't decided to chance you still being up—I realise now that you're always going to attract the male gender, but I don't intend to stand around and watch it happen. I'm sorry—more than you know—but I don't think we can either of us change anything. I made a mistake—that's all.'

He walked to the door. 'Goodbye. I don't expect we shall meet again, but—good luck—in whatever you do. And if it's any consolation—you are the only woman I have ever wanted for my wife. The mother of my children—but I daresay I can do without either, if I have to.'

She had kept her face hidden from him. She couldn't speak because of the tears choking her, so he left quietly, having delivered the last crushing blow; and she heard the door close behind him.

Perhaps his utter rejection of her in some way made it a little easier. Because at some time he would discover the truth and this sorrow and regret would be his too. But it would all be too late. They could never recapture the timeless joy of those first days of discovered love for each other; finding that one thing together. There would be others—but that had been too perfect ever to replace.

Yet, intuition told her that his shattering conclusions were directed at her only because he had been deeply hurt, believing that she had behaved badly with a younger man, and suffering just as she was, with an even more bruised ego. Yet, even today, while he was deliberately causing her more pain to ease his own, one good look into her eyes, which mirrored her very soul in the stark agony of it all—and he would have known, seen the truth, that she loved him and he was wounding her unmercifully. Just at a time when she was not equipped to defend herself—or chose not to. But he hadn't done that.

A deputation of nurses arrived at eight that evening with a bottle of champagne and a leaving present of two very elegant matching pieces of luggage for which they had collected.

It was almost more than she could take, but she didn't have to hide her emotion from them. They accepted her weak tears as post-flu depression, except Jenny, who knew the true reason. But even she hadn't been told of Duncan's visit that afternoon.

The day before Elizabeth was coming to fetch her, Jenny helped her pack her things. She still felt far from well and while it meant a long drive for her stepmother, she was unutterably relieved that she was going to Cornwall by road. If anyone could help her over this traumatic period, Elizabeth would; and for the first time since she had left home she really needed that help. Her illness could not have come at a worse time.

For the first part of the journey she couldn't trust herself to speak and Elizabeth, concentrating on driving along the motorways, didn't press her. If she had been shocked at the change in Meryl she didn't comment, except to say that the sooner she got her home, the sooner she would feel better.

Which had to be true. Because, as they covered the miles, Meryl accepted that there was no chance of seeing Duncan again and now their parting was complete: the end, reached and passed. That door on her life was closed now. Everything she did in future would be a new phase and already Elizabeth had hinted that she had a proposition in mind when she felt up to talking about it.

'What is it?'

'Oh, not now, love. Perhaps in a few days—when you're rested up—there's no immediate hurry. Just relax—close your eyes—we'll soon be home.'

Obediently she did just that and the quiet humming of the engine lulled her into sleep, so that when she awoke they were coming up to the gates of Bay Trees. Never had she been more pleased to see the house which was home to her now.

The next days were ones of complete rest and quiet with no responsibility, and time in which to recover her strength. But the sadness in her eyes, the mental lethargy—was another matter and presented a much more difficult hill to climb. Until Elizabeth jolted her out of it one evening after supper.

'How would you like to go to Canada for a month or two, Meryl?' she asked brightly.

'Me? Canada?' Meryl repeated incredulously.

'Why not you?' Elizabeth said firmly. 'I'm looking for someone to accompany one of my patients out to BC to her son and his family and stay long enough to settle her in and get her properly mobile before leaving her there on a permanent basis. All expenses will be met, of course, and Mr Hunter has offered a good salary while you are there with them. I gather it's a kind of farming background. You'd probably enjoy it.' She went on making notes on the pad on her knee while Meryl sat silently thinking. Now Elizabeth stopped, her pen poised, while she regarded her seriously. 'Don't you think this might be just the opportunity you need right now?' she asked gently. 'A breathing space? After you come back you can look around and choose something which furthers your career, if that's what you want. You might even consider private nursing. That is very remunerative . . .'

'No . . .' Meryl shook her head. 'I don't think I want

to do that. Not permanently anyway; but this Canadian proposition—well that's something else.' She looked up, the first glimmer of interest reflected on her face. 'When would I have to go?'

'In two weeks if Mrs Hunter's son can make all the arrangements. I think the flight is already booked tentatively.'

'Two weeks. It isn't long to finalise everything, but . . .'

'You do have a current passport?'

'Yes.' The pain in her chest erupted without warning at her words. They were the ones Duncan had used when they had talked of their honeymoon. He had been going to plan it all as a surprise. Now, with the memory still fresh in her mind, the decision was made. It was what she needed, the chance to get right away, to a new environment, new experiences, even new customs. It was an attractive thought and, for the first time, she began to want to think of clothes and make a few plans of her own. She had to start looking forward and not back.

Elizabeth put a call through to Mr Hunter that same night and it was all arranged. When she came back she poured them a glass of sherry each. 'Go on—drink it—you need some colour in your cheeks. We'll go out tomorrow and walk along the cliff tops—I'll soon have you back in circulation once you get your appetite back.'

'Oh—what would I do without you?' Meryl looked at her wistfully. 'I feel as if I've been dragged through a fishing net. It's been rather a ghastly time, Elizabeth. I know I haven't told you what really happened—only that—everything is off between Duncan and me, but not why. Do you mind?'

'If you don't want to talk about it,' Elizabeth said bluntly, 'then don't. But you must think of yourself.

Your future—and I think this trip has come in good time for you to do just that. But first—you do have to be really fit again. So—we start tomorrow. Then you can get right into it. What about clothes? It will be May when you arrive and Mr Hunter says it is still a bit on the chilly side. June is the warmer month so you'll need woollies and a few lighter things then.' She smiled warmly. 'You'll be able to use your new luggage.'

But this only conjured up memories of the day when Duncan came to the flat—and Meryl didn't reply. She only knew that she was grasping this new opportunity like a straw in the wind, thankful that it had come just at the right time.

The flight was long and because she had the responsibility of looking after her elderly patient, Meryl was more concerned for her than herself. But she stood the journey very well and slept most of the time, while Meryl could only gaze down on to breath-taking views of ocean and ice floes and, high above the clouds, sunlit blue skies, until at last they were flying over the snow-covered Canadian Rockies and now Mrs Hunter too began to feel the excitement of seeing her family again, even if she did voice her qualms at leaving the old country for good.

'You'll be fine,' Meryl told her comfortingly. 'I am sure it will be the best tonic you can have. Your son is coming to meet you at Vancouver Airport you know, so once we arrive there your troubles are over.'

Mine too—she thought a little nervously, because there was still quite a journey after that by road and she wouldn't be really happy until her patient was tucked up in bed and resting. Air Canada had provided a wheelchair which meant they were first off the plane. It was raining as they went into the terminal and very noisy, and even she felt the exhaustion of jet lag sapping her strength as she coped with the chair and their hand luggage and customs; then waited for their bags to come from the plane before getting them taken out to the arrival foyer while she followed.

Suddenly, everything was taken out of her hands when a Canadian voice behind her said strongly, 'Hullo, there. I see you've brought my mother here safely.' Then he was bending to hug the old lady in the chair and Meryl could only watch the two heads close together for a moment. One fair, with slightly greying hair; the other, fragile, soft silver wisps, creeping under the fur hat which he had knocked slightly awry. His toughened weathered face contrasting against the delicate skin of his mother, but the tears were happy ones and Meryl waited until they were over and it was time to move out to the waiting car to take them out beyond the mountains to his home in the Canadian backwoods.

The car was huge by any standards and he had thoughtfully provided pillows and rugs so that she could make Mrs Hunter comfortable on the back seat, sitting with her because, even now, she wasn't sure that the excitement and arduous journey from Cornwall to halfway across the world wouldn't prove too much for her. But she could still marvel at the little she saw of Vancouver city as they passed through; the backcloth of mountains, deep snow still on their peaks reflecting the myriad of colours from the rays of the setting sun disappearing behind soaring skyscrapers to the West. Clive Hunter spoke occasionally, pointing out various landmarks, but already the lights were coming on all over the city in their thousands and as they took the highway leading up through the suburbs and out towards the even higher mountains in the distance, she felt brainwashed by the bright lights and neon signs flashing constantly, relieved to be leaving the mass of traffic behind.

'Is it far to where we are going?' she asked after he had switched on more powerful lights when they plunged into darkness between the mountains.

'A fair way . . .' he threw over his shoulder. 'Do I call you Nurse—by the way?'

She laughed softly, not to waken Mrs Hunter. 'I shouldn't think so. Meryl will do.'

'Good. Well, we have a couple of hundred kilometres yet, I guess. So why not have a nap too. It's a pity because you would have enjoyed the scenery during the day time through here. But I guess you may come this way again some time. Nothing to see now but those peaks up there and they look a bit hostile tonight. At least it's stopped raining.'

'I am amazed at the vast distances between towns. I hadn't realised it was such a long way from the airport,' she said quietly.

'Oh—we shall be there before eleven o'clock, I guess, so you'll get a good night's sleep before having a look round the place tomorrow. When you've travelled over six thousand miles this last bit is minimal.'

'I wouldn't say that exactly. It's just a bit awe-inspiring though. Do you have any neighbours?'

'Yea. The Rogers family aren't too far and the Cavells—just the other side of the river. We think nothing of driving fifty kilometres to a party. That's about the size of our social life—what we make of it. I hope Mother won't find it too lonely. 'It's forty miles to the stores.'

'Not when she is with her family.'

Quiet came when he thought she was asleep too and there was only the purr of tyres on the asphalt roads as the wheels traversed the miles, occasionally passing a house or two, a few farm buildings, but mainly nothing that she could see other than trees, darker than the night.

It was a kind of transient phase of finding herself between two places; the one she knew—England, home, the hospital, Duncan—and the one she didn't ahead of her. Everything was going to be quite new, untrodden ground. She had to get used to new customs, a new way of life. It was a challenge and might even be quite enjoyable. If his family was as easy to talk to as Clive Hunter, she need have no misgivings.

Which proved to be the case. For after a warm welcome and more tears from Mrs Hunter as she saw her grandchildren again for the first time in years, and a hearth glowing with logs like tree trunks where they sat for a little while in the huge family room, they talked excitedly until Meryl, seeing her effort to keep conversing, suggested that she should take her to bed.

Two rooms had been prepared at the end of the low wood ranch house which, furnished in the homely old colonial style, was exactly the way Meryl saw it. A real home. She knew that Mrs Hunter couldn't fail to be happy here—there was enough room for privacy when she wanted it, yet never again would she be completely lonely.

She settled at once and Meryl at last escaped to her own room, but sleep was a long time in coming because, in England now, they would already be getting into the morning routine at the hospital and Duncan would— oh—no . . . She must stop this. But somehow so far away—she was seeing it all in a kind of separate perspective. Outside, looking in and she knew that she was missing him all over again. That his face only was the one face she looked for and would, every day of her life probably. Would they ever see each other again? Because she still loved him and there was nothing she could do about it, no matter how many miles she put between them.

CHAPTER SEVEN

THE Hunters measured up to Meryl's first impressions of them. They were warm and easy to live with, and each day was far less pressured than she had envisaged.

Her patient too was soon integrated into her new surroundings and greatly comforted that her family were no longer thousands of miles away but at close range where she could see them every day.

Julie, a student nurse at a hospital in Hundred Mile House, a small town, originally one of the mile post houses on the Cariboo wagon trail in the early fur and gold rush days, had come home especially to welcome her grandmother, while Paul, at twenty, worked with his father running the farm. Louise, their mother, just thrived on looking after the home and family and entertaining their friends. Social life was never dull. Everyone seemed to come and go on an open-house basis and Meryl's stay seemed almost a holiday after the pressures and close timing of the hospital routine she was used to.

The early summer days were golden, with the sun on the wheat and the corn-cobs in the fields growing fast in the mixture of rain and warmth. There were long, balmy evenings and an enormous sense of space whenever she got away from the house for a short time.

She still thought about Duncan a lot, but now she could accept the fact that he was a part of her life that had gone for ever. It was hard to adjust to that, but it was true. She even began toying with the idea of staying on in Canada for a while when she left her patient; and she saved most of her salary with this in mind. Besides which, there was nothing to spend it on so far out of town.

The improvement in Mrs Hunter was tremendous as she persevered with her physiotherapy and after only two weeks she was no longer confirmed to her wheel-chair but walking, very slowly it was true, with the help of an aid to lean on.

Meryl had actually got her out of the house and on to the patio where there was shelter from the sun one afternoon and, seeing that she was having a nap, stretch-ed out herself on a lounge chair a little distance away, letting the new warmth ease the muscles of her body under her cotton sun dress, green and white, cool and fresh. She didn't know that Sean Rogers never forgot the way she looked that day when, seeing her for the first time, sun-kissed and lightly tanned, he came looking for Paul. He stood, quite still, assessing her as he would a new acquisition in the animal field, as she lay there.

'Gee . . .' he murmured, 'What am I waiting for? She's something . . .'

So it was that Meryl, opening her eyes, stared straight up into his suntanned face as he stood beside her chair. He was very fair and young and virile. He seemed to exude virility and she sat up quickly, aware of this.

'Hi, there—sleeping beauty,' he said teasingly, his smile widening into a white teeth-showing grin. 'Paul didn't tell me about you. I can see why now.'

Meryl got up off the chair, then, straightening her dress and giving her patient a swift glance to assure herself that she still dozed peacefully, she said quietly,

'I'm sorry. I'm afraid I don't . . .'

'I'm Sean Rogers,' he said softly so as not to waken Mrs Hunter either, because he wanted this lovely English rose to himself for a bit longer. 'Who are you?'

'Meryl Summers. I'm Mrs Hunter's nurse. I'm afraid everyone is out.'

'That's okay, Meryl. I can easily call Paul this evening. How long are you going to stay here?' He regarded her thoughtfully, his head on one side, waiting for an answer.

'I really don't know, Mr Rogers.'

'Oh, Sean, please. We don't stand on ceremony over here. Well—it's sure nice to have you around and I'll be seeing you again. That sun looks good on you. Bye now.'

He threw her an intimate glance with eyes sparkling and smiling behind their blueness, so that she always remembered the vividness of them and, turning away, heard his car start up at once, zooming away out of earshot. It wakened Mrs Hunter which Meryl hadn't wanted to happen, preferring to do it quietly if she had to rouse her.

That same evening when Sean phoned, Paul looked across the room to where she was helping unravel the old lady's knitting; good therapy for her weakened arm. His slow, Canadian drawl reached her, making her look round quickly.

'Meryl—you're invited to Sean's barbecue on Saturday. I can take you with me. Do you want to go?'

He saw her hesitation. 'I'm not free to go, Paul. But thank him for the invitation.'

'Of course you are. That's if you want to,' Louise said firmly, coming into the room. 'We shall be here. You don't mind, do you, Mother?'

'No . . . She should get out and meet people. I can go to bed beforehand if it will help?' She smiled at Meryl.

'So—you'll come?' Paul asked, still patiently waiting with the phone in his hand.

'Yes, then. Thanks. I'd like to.'

She heard his, 'Okay, Sean. I'll bring her along with me. Yes—fine—about eight. Okay—we'll be there . . .'

Soon after that she took her patient to bed, staying in her own room afterwards to write some letters, leaving the family to watch television or relax without intrusion, which she considered important after the way they had changed their home and lifestyle to accommodate Mrs Hunter and herself so unselfishly. But a little smile curved her lips because Sean had phoned to invite her specially. It was good to have her ego pandered to, just a little, after the hurtful things that had been said by Duncan of all people, bruising it so badly.

It was a lovely summer evening when she drove off beside Paul across country to the ranch where Sean lived with his parents. They were giving their barbecue evening for no special reason as far as Meryl knew, but she had wanted to look right and was undecided what to wear, asking Mrs Hunter's advice.

Her yellow soft cotton blouse with tiny frills at the neck and sleeves and a matching full skirt proved to be just right, with flat sandals of leather to tone. Her hair, healthy and shining without the restrictions of her uniform cap, caught the reflections of the sun as they drove along off-beat roads and lanes leading to the Rogers' ranch at the end of a huge lake edged with dark green spruce trees. Already there were boats and numerous landing stages along the way, and the nearer they came to the house, gleaming white among the trees, the more she felt as if she had been lifted from one environment and simply dropped here into another.

The open ranges on her left stretched away to the hills. There were cattle as far as the eye could see, already on their summer grazing wanderings.

'They'll travel for the next few months,' Paul explained, 'until the fall round-up when they'll be brought back here. It's a good life, isn't it? If you like the elements.'

'The ranch house looks very prosperous,' she observed. 'Are the Rogers very wealthy people?'

'I guess so—in a way. Gee—just look at that sunset.'

The white-tipped mountains a long way off were glorious in the reflection of the golden sun, tinged with slashes of flame as it began its descent in the west behind them.

'It's quite spectacular,' Meryl sat gazing across the trees towards it at the splendour nature had conjured up for her tonight. And now they came to the lakeside. Cars were lined up and Paul, leaning forward as he parked beside them, said with pleasure in his voice,

'Ah—there's Abby. Over there—the girl in green. I'll introduce you. She's—kind of special.'

'Your girl friend, Paul?'

'She sure is. Quite a party, isn't it?'

Meryl followed him across the grass to the girl coming eagerly towards them.

'Abby—this is Meryl,' he said, throwing an arm around her shoulders. 'Where is Sean?'

'Right here,' a laughing voice replied as he came to join them, casting an admiring glance over Meryl, obviously liking what he saw, before taking her arm and leading her over to the drinks table where a group of other guests were assembled.

'I want you to meet my parents,' he told her quite seriously. 'After that, we'll circulate. There'll be dancing later. I'm glad you came, Meryl.'

His parents greeted her with the same friendly casualness she had come to associate with the locality and as the evening progressed she really began to enjoy the whole thing.

Huge steaks spluttered on the barbecue grids and as

darkness descended the coloured lights strewn between
the trees came on, reflecting in the calm lake water
lapping gently on its shores. She was glad to have her
wool coat as she wandered with Sean along its edge.
While there was an undercurrent of ill-concealed need
for a closer, even more intimate thing between them, he
accepted her reticence, even withdrawal, and his light-
hearted banter soon shook her right out of the de-
spondency she had been living with since Duncan had
gone out of her life. Would she ever feel completely
whole again? Ever be able to give her love again? How
could she tell? Not yet anyway—she was unmoved by
Sean's obvious attraction towards her. Emotions were
too raw, even if they were embedded in her heart.
Neither did she want to replace what Duncan still meant
to her. Perhaps she never would be able to.

'Enjoying yourself, honey?' Sean's voice invaded her
musings as they turned to go back to where the music
had started and couples were dancing on an improvised
floor in a clearing.

'Yes—yes I am.' It was suddenly true. For too long she
had not been really alive. And tonight—there was everything for enjoyment. She was young enough to appreci-
ate the atmosphere of good food and wine and music and
dancing. The smell of coffee, the warmth and hospital-
ity; the freedom—as Sean led her towards the floor and
put his arms around her. And all around the trees
quivered in the soft night breezes and the mountains
stood silently sentinel beyond the lakeside, and there
was laughter, gay voices and fun, even happiness. A
night to remember . . .

Dancing with Sean, the wine making her a little muzzy
now, she looked vainly for Paul, but he seemed to have
disappeared. Sean knew at once, asking solicitously,
'Do you want to go, Meryl?' and when she nodded he led

her off the floor, holding on to her hand.

'I can't see Paul . . .' she said.

'I guess not. I'm taking you back anyway.'

'Oh . . . are you?'

'You don't object?'

'Of course not. But—can we go soon? It's after twelve.'

'Sure. Right now, honey.'

'But I must first thank your parents for a lovely evening.'

'They've already gone into the house,' he assured her. 'Besides, it's my party and you can say thank you to me,' he smiled disarmingly, leaving her a little disconcerted as she got into his yellow convertible. His legs touched hers as he slid into the bucket seat beside her and the next moment it shot forward, taking the long drive through which she had come with Paul at break-neck speed as the darkness swallowed them up.

The wind blew through her hair, deliciously cool on her heated cheeks after the wine and the dancing and the hilarious fun of the party. She had enjoyed it very much; a kind of release from the tightness which had been with her for the past weeks. But as they traversed the gravel roads until they reached a smoother highway she had to hold on because Sean's driving was a little reckless. More than once as they rounded a bend he was leaning on her, so that by the time the farm buildings came into view, the dutch barn a shape at the end of the lane, she was biting her lips nervously again.

With a sigh of relief she saw that a light was still on in the porch, but even before the car stopped with a scrunch of tyres on the gravel, Sean's arm slipped around her shoulders, his hand expertly turning her face to his, reaching to kiss her, so swiftly she had no time to object. Curiously, she assessed her own response, staying passive under his hot, searching mouth. There was no point in struggling and she was adult too, wasn't she? But it was just a 'thank you' kiss she left him with, as she disentangled herself and reached for the door handle decisively.

'I have to go in now, Sean. But thanks again. It was a lovely evening.'

'Must you go?' he groaned.

'Yes. Goodnight . . .'

'Okay,' he said resignedly, 'but we'll do it again—won't we? Tomorrow?'

Laughingly she shook her head. 'Not tomorrow. I'm here to look after my patient. Remember?'

He let her go then, waiting until she had gone into the house before driving off.

Meryl was wondering how she was going to keep him at some sort of distance because, although he was fun to be with, she was not going to get involved again, even if she wanted to, which she didn't.

As she came to the bedrooms, Louise opened her door softly and came out, wearing a blue housecoat. Putting her fingers to her lips so that they wouldn't waken Mrs Hunter, Senior, she led Meryl back into the lounge, switching on the wall lights. Meryl had already sensed that something was wrong.

'What is it?' she asked quickly.

'You had a phone call. From your stepmother.'

'Elizabeth? Please tell me . . . It isn't . . .' For an awful moment she thought of Duncan. An accident . . .

Louise saw her face whiten. 'It's your uncle . . .' she said quietly. 'I am afraid he has died. They live in the Hebrides—is that right?'

'Uncle Lewis, yes. Oh—poor Aunt Bea—when?'

'I'm not sure. But I promised your stepmother that you would phone her when you returned.'

'Tonight? Isn't it too late? Oh—of course it will already be morning in England. I'll do it now. Thank you for waiting up. I was trying not to wake you.' Meryl was still trying to cope with shock.

'I heard the car. Now—you call your stepmother and I'll make some fresh coffee. Would you like some brandy?'

'No, thank you. Why don't you go back to bed? I'll make some coffee after I've talked to Elizabeth.'

'No. I expect you'll want to talk a little. It's rather an anticlimax, isn't it?'

It was amazing just to pick up the phone, dial the numbers and almost before she took another breath, hear it ringing at Bay Trees and Elizabeth's voice asking how she was feeling now before giving her more news of her uncle's death in the hospital on Skye.

'The funeral is tomorrow, so there is no way either of us can be there, and your Aunt didn't want us to try. He has been ailing for weeks so it wasn't entirely unexpected.'

'Oh, dear. How does Aunt Bea seem?'

'Apparently she hasn't been too well herself. It's a bit worrying—so far away.'

'Maybe I could break my journey when I come home and go over to spend a few days with her.'

'What a good idea. Stop off at Prestwick, you mean?'

'Yes. Mrs Hunter is progressing so well that I shall soon be able to leave her. Do I hear the tea cups rattling in the background?'

'You do. It's after breakfast here. And you've been to a party I'm told . . .'

'A barbecue actually. I'll tell you about it when I write. Thank you for calling, Elizabeth. It's good to hear you.'

'Sorry it wasn't better news, love. Come back soon. I miss you.'

'Me too.'

She hadn't expected to sleep because of the events and thoughts churning around in her brain after they had eventually gone to bed. And it was still not four a.m. when she got up and watched the first pink glow of dawn in the sky. And by then she had reached a decision. When next she took Mrs Hunter for physiotherapy she would ask about leaving her for the family to supervise now. After that, she slept at once, wakened by the old lady buzzing her for her early morning orange juice. But Meryl felt that her own family needed her now, so she set about persuading her patient to do a little more for herself so that she would not be too much of a burden here when she went away. Suddenly she was very home-sick for England.

Strangely, the Hunter family had been discussing the same proposition and when she asked to speak with them both that evening they discussed the situation fully.

Also, there was the financial angle to be considered. Now that their mother was so much better, she didn't really need a full-time nurse at the salary they were paying Meryl, although they would never have dreamed of bringing up the subject if she hadn't. It was time to go. So it was agreed that as soon as she could get a flight the family would take over the care of her patient.

'Julie will be home soon for a vacation before she goes to Vancouver for further training,' Louise said as an afterthought. 'Oh—we shall manage between us. You do just what you want now, Meryl. We are eternally grateful for all that you've done for Mother.'

So she phoned the airport at Vancouver and was given

a reservation on a flight to Prestwick, Scotland in two weeks' time.

Sean was visually rumpled at her news when he arrived without warning and, to the amusement of Paul and Louise, insisted that she couldn't possibly go away yet.

'You've only just got here. Besides, what about that trip you were going to take—see Canada, you said. You can't let that up. I'd even thought of coming with you.'

Her eyes opened wide at that. But she didn't intimidate him by saying how impossible a suggestion that would have been. Her voice was gentle as she explained. 'It's family, Sean. My aunt was there when I needed her, while I was still at school. She tried to take my mother's place after she died, and now, she needs help. I have to go and visit her.'

'Okay. But I'll be around. Guess I'll just have to pull out all the stops where you're concerned, Meryl. I want you; and I usually get what I want.'

She recognised undertones which she refused to take seriously. But she must certainly play it cool and give him no encouragement during her time here at the farm. She didn't want to hurt him; he was a generous and likeable boy, but not for her.

Meryl wrote off to her aunt immediately and when a letter arrived back she was even more certain that her decision to go and see her was the right one. In fact, there was an element of unrest at the delay before she could get there. Something in her aunt's letter was rather worrying, because she was certainly far from well.

Neither did she know what to expect on the island. She had simply a rough idea of where she lived, alone in her croft up in the hills. But she would find it, the challenge was already reaching out to her.

When her flight time was confirmed, it was Sean who insisted on driving her into Vancouver International Airport. She couldn't refuse his offer, especially as he said that he had business to attend to on that day. And it would let Paul out, because it was a busy time out of doors just then and Clive Hunter was up early and working until late most days out on his land too. It would mean taking a whole day off.

So she accepted gratefully, if a little uncomfortably, because, of late, she had avoided Sean where possible.

'If you're sure it won't be out of your way,' she said hesitantly.

'No problem,' he grinned. 'There is just no way you're going back to the UK without someone seeing you off. I just wish you were staying over here, but I guess you know that, don't you, honey?'

'Sean, I really am sorry, but . . .'

He smiled ruefully. 'I know. I guess I don't make the bells ring for you. Just wish I had more time to work at it. Maybe, then, you might just listen for them . . .'

She shook her head. 'No. I don't think it happens like that,' she said positively.

He tilted her determined little chin, looking deep into the dark fringed eyes which met his honestly, then moved his hands to her waist. She stood quite still, resisting their pressure and he gave up. But twisting a dark brown curl of her hair between his fingers as she broke away, he lifted it to his lips, then let her go, before walking quickly away.

He hadn't come to the farm again until the party on her last night which the Hunters had arranged for her. And next day he arrived in good time, stacking her cases into the back of his car while she said her final goodbyes. Then they were driving away between the corn fields and out towards the hills. She was on her way back home.

Sean was a fast, risk-taking driver which she knew already, but now it certainly didn't contribute to her enjoyment of the journey. Neither did the weather. A storm came in swiftly from the mountains and it was the worst storm in density that Meryl had ever experienced.

There were angry streaks of fiery red in the darkened clouds, indigo and grey behind the mountains on either side of the highway, and thunder still rumbled through the valleys, echoing eerily. There was little traffic and she felt they could have been the only two people in the world in a kind of Hades; their faces red and green in a new spectacular sweep of colour across the sky.

Sean leaned over the wheel of the car to cast a speculative glance up at the sky before changing into the fast lane.

'I guess we're leaving that little display of nature behind us now,' he observed, 'and any moment you'll see Vancouver signposted. Are you okay?'

'Yes. But it was certainly frightening,' Meryl mused, relaxing once more.

'It's always fierce up here among the sprawling ruggedness of the Rockies,' he said. 'The storm gets in and can't get out again, I guess.'

'You've an answer for everything,' she smiled slightly, feeling more relaxed now.

'For most things . . .' he admitted shamelessly.

But after endless driving he heard her almost imperceptible sigh of relief as the first mountain peaks and tall skyscrapers of Vancouver were sighted. And out there the sun sparkled on to a deep blue sea and, suddenly, it was summer again. Now they were dropping down into the teeming city roads, crowded with slow-moving traffic and the frustration began to build up because she had a plane to catch. Here were the neon lights and blocks of buildings belonging to another world from the slower way of life in the farming areas. But they crossed the bridge at last and the airport too was sign-posted now. She sat up and drew a deep breath.

'There's a plane just coming in,' Sean told her, 'and you can see the terminal buildings now. You'll make it in good time.'

'It didn't seem so long when I came over,' she replied. 'I'd forgotten how far it really is to the farm.'

'Yet you came this same route.'

'I know. But I was concerned for my patient then and didn't see very much. It was a long journey for her by road after the flight and I wasn't sure we weren't expecting too much from her. But she so much wanted to see her family again. It was worth it, as it happens.'

'And she's made a good recovery. Thanks to you.'

'Oh—it was because of them. It helped enormously that they made her welcome.'

'And your expert nursing, of course, I noticed that . . .'

She flashed him a grateful look. It was nice to be appreciated. Sean could be so likeable when he was being serious. Besides—she had to admit his wild, good looks, those rougish eyes he used for getting his own way. Any girl would notice them.

They were already drawing up in front of the terminal entrance and he was out of the car at once and depositing her luggage on the pavement. Then he opened her door and held his hand out for her, his blue eyes more expressive than ever, so that she wondered what was so funny. She held out her hand.

'This is goodbye then, Sean,' she began, but he stop-ped her.

'You just wait here, honey, while I park the car, then I'll be right back.'

Her face registered surprise. 'But don't you have an

appointment? I'm quite able to see myself off.'

He grinned mischievously. 'There is always time for business, that's for sure, but I'd rather be with you. So—you just wait, right there.'

When he didn't return after a few minutes, Meryl, with an eye on the clock, decided to go on into the departure hall to arrange about her boarding pass and her seat which she wanted next to a window, if possible. Besides which, she knew how unpredictable Sean could be; anything could delay him. A pretty girl for instance.

So she resolutely picked up her two cases and struggled inside where the noise and buzzing and voices over the intercom just went on over her head. He would know where to look for her. Besides, seating on the DC10, Air Canada flight to Prestwick and London was being taken up quite fast. Soon it was her turn and as she watched her bags disappear after the weigh-in, she breathed a sigh of relief. She was on her way. Back home—back to where Duncan was. Impatient now to return. Picking up her boarding pass and tickets she was stuck for words as Sean dashed up to the desk, blatantly jumping the queue, and planting two bags on the scales before handing a ticket to the Air Canada girl behind the desk.

'We're travelling together,' he explained disarmingly to the other passengers, fully aware of their eyebrows raised in protest. 'I got delayed a little.' It paid off, as he knew it would, and when he joined Meryl he simply laughed at her surprise. But she was trying to come to terms with the fact that he was actually coming on the flight with her.

'I just don't believe it,' she said, shaking her head as he waved his tickets at her. 'You really do have nerve enough for anything. And you get away with it. So—do you mean to tell me that you're going to Scotland too?'

'I sure am, honey. I wasn't telling you a lie either. I did

have business here in Vancouver, arranging about my car and paying for my ticket which I ordered by phone last week. But you're supposed to look surprised, overjoyed at having my company on the flight. It was a well-kept secret because everyone knew back there, except you.'

While they stood side by side going up the escalator, she said drily, 'We'd better go straight into the departure lounge. It's almost time to board. Then you can tell me about it. It was certainly a well-kept secret, because I hadn't a clue.'

When they were sitting in the yellow armchairs, she crossed one elegantly shoed leg over the other, regarding him coolly, while she waited for him to tell her about his plans.

'You knew it was on the cards that I would be going to Scotland this year, didn't you?'

She shook her head. 'No . . .'

'Oh, sure. We have family there. I shall be staying with an uncle who farms near Oban and another has a herd of Highland cattle further north. My father wants to start the same strain in Canada. So I'm over there to look into it.' He threw her a teasing glance. 'I've also got a very attractive Scots cousin I haven't seen yet. Jealous?' he looked at her hopefully.

'Not in the least,' she affirmed truthfully, but knowing that his conceit would never allow him to believe it, even though her eyes met his calmly and didn't waver.

Their flight was called then which was something of a relief. Actually, Meryl was dismayed that he would be sitting next to her all those hours. She had intended using them to get some ordered planning into her future. She had simply been going through a readjusting period after Duncan had gone out of her life, leaving it empty.

She had been like a small boat, rudderless on a stormy

sea. Now, for the first time, away from the confines and routine of the busy Hunter family, she had no more responsibility. She was free. It had been a kind of therapy. It had helped her forget. But now—she only wanted to remember—now that she could cope, without tears. She didn't hurt so much. She could see his love for her in perspective; just not able to stand up to any strains. It would never have survived because of his jealousy. So—perhaps it was a good thing that it was behind her. But it must not be allowed to ruin the rest of her life—she had to make a fresh start. But where? She was all set to find herself again, pick up the pieces of her broken romance—oh—it was much more than that.

And walking beside Sean now, going up into the aircraft, she knew that her moment of truth would have to be delayed; she would have to socialise all the way across the Atlantic to Scotland. No dreaming on this trip, not with Sean in the seat next to hers.

Fastening her seat belt she sighed deeply as the lights flashed on and the plane got ready for take off.

'You're not nervous, are you?' he asked, noticing how quiet she had become.

'Oh, no. I enjoy flying.' She did in fact feel far safer than in the car to the airport.

'So . . .' he went on, as they started to climb. 'What are your plans when you get to Scotland? I suppose there is no chance they could include me?'

'No . . .' Meryl had to smile in spite of herself. He was incorrigible, especially when he wore that hang-dog look.

'Are you going back to hospital work?'

'Oh—definitely. But not immediately. I shall go straight to the Isle of Skye where my aunt lives, then back to Cornwall and, after that, I'll start looking seriously.'

'Will you give me your address while you're in Scotland?'

She couldn't see anything wrong in that so she wrote it down for him and his spirits rose as the drinks trolley began to make its way down between the seats. He guessed there had been a man in Meryl's life who had temporarily turned her off men, leaving some disillusionment, even bitterness. He had tried to overcome her lack of response to his bizarre efforts to make her fall for his own charms. Without success. And he had jumped at his father's suggestion to take some time in Scotland and find out about their kind of cattle. Something might be accomplished with Meryl too. You never could tell—he had nothing to lose after all, and much to gain. Because she had really got to him; this green-eyed girl he wanted for his own, her reticence an added incentive.

The Fraser River, threading between the canyons far below them, roared endlessly on to the sea and, as they flew south, Meryl gazed down over the mountains and lakes, like tiny mirrors among the spruce forests, on over vast areas of wheat and the thriving city of Edmonton; listening to the plane's engines, taking her home.

She couldn't wait to see the rugged coast of Cornwall again, the tiny farms and white cottages, the summer roses. But not yet. First stop, Scotland. Oh—if only Duncan had been waiting for her there. But he was walking the hospital wards miles from Scotland, watching over his patients, working to make them well. That was his life. And she was no longer a part of it. She had to start a new life somewhere else.

Meryl didn't hear when Sean asked what she was dreaming about. When he leaned forward to see her face, she turned away; there were tears in the eyes which gazed down at the dazzling, sunlit peaks below and she didn't want him to see them.

Very early in the morning as they finished eating breakfast, after a night when they had dozed from sheer exhaustion, he asked suddenly, 'How do you intend getting to the Hebrides? By plane?'

'Heavens, no. Train I should think. Then a short trip across the sea to Skye. After that, I'm hazy. Bus—if there is one—or car. It depends how far it is. I believe Aunt Bea said once that it's a bit inaccessible.'

'No-one to meet you . . . ?'

'Afraid not. They didn't have a car but went everywhere by bicycle.'

'It's unfortunate that I shall be going in the opposite direction. I'm being met. I wonder if we could take you somewhere. I guess so.'

'No, thank you, Sean. Don't feel responsible for me,' she assured him positively.

'You'll keep in touch, honey? Here's my phone number. Do you have one?'

'I—don't think so.'

He gave up then and they both looked interestedly down at the scattered islands dotted around the Scottish coast, seemingly uninhabited except for a few sheep. The plane began its descent after hovering in mid air for the signal to come in to land. Then the wheels were grinding on the soaked runway and Meryl got into her yellow raincoat. She had worn a cream cotton suit to travel in and narrow strapped sandals. After all, it was summertime, but not here. The early morning was surprisingly chilly as they stepped down into puddles of rain water and she wished she had changed her shoes before this.

Ahead of them, passengers from a scheduled flight from London were already going through into the terminal.

'Ugh . . .' she shuddered, closing up to Sean, who had

an arm around her shoulders to shield her a little. 'After that lovely weather we've just left—this is ghastly. Not much of a welcome for you, I'm afraid.'

He pulled her against his shoulder, smiling down into her upturned face. 'I don't mind.' The rain made his fair hair curl. Very attractively, she thought, as she began to notice that other girls were eyeing him as they waited to go through customs. He was, however, behaving rather possessively towards her, as if they were something more to each other; perhaps just to impress the tall, burly Scotsman who was obviously searching for somebody.

'Hi, there . . .' Sean shouted across the hall, turning more than one head to see who was so impetuous. He was recognised and the smiles were much in evidence, especially when he pulled Meryl forward and introduced her.

When their luggage was cleared she said that she must make some enquiries. 'So this is goodbye . . .'

'Oh—not yet, honey.' And now as they all emerged together, everyone talking at the same time, she had to insist that she was perfectly capable of finding her own way. As it happened, Sean's uncle directed her. It would be by train and he offered to get her to the station.

'You'll go across to Skye by ferry—it's a short journey. After that, I'm not sure.'

'Okay . . .' she agreed. 'That's very good of you.' As Sean's uncle had gone to fetch the Range Rover nearer to the terminal entrance, Sean took advantage of that, kissing her upturned face, reluctant to let her go.

'Oh, Sean, behave . . .' she said crossly, then stopped, unable to move. A man with reddish-brown hair was finishing his coffee, his back to the window. The eyes meeting hers were unreadable, but resigned.

'Duncan . . .' she whispered, wanting to run into his

arms, burrow into them, shut out every single thing but each other. She didn't question why he was here as she stood, rooted to the spot, her heart hammering in her chest the way it always had.

He made no move towards her, his iron will holding him back. Then, glancing at his watch, he put his cup and saucer carefully down on to the table, picked up his raincoat and walked slowly but determinedly away from her, towards the exit leading out to the airfield.

'Oh—no—no . . .' she groaned silently, 'don't go away again . . .'

Without realising what she did, she went over to the wide window, watching his upright figure in the beige suit, carrying only his raincoat and a bag, heading for the small plane on the runway. He climbed into it and it took off at once. Soon it was a speck on the edge of the dark clouds. And she turned to see Sean beckoning to her from the doorway. Like a zombie she went out and got into the Range Rover, puzzled as to Duncan's movements, hurt beyond description again at his dismissal of her. Couldn't he just have said 'Hullo'? He thought she was with Sean, of course. Had seen his kiss, his monopolising of her. Known too that they had come in on the same Canadian flight. He thought she had consoled herself with yet another man. That he had been right in his decision to end everything between them.

CHAPTER EIGHT

MERYL sat gazing out of the window at the breath-taking scenery of the Highlands as the train sped northwards. After travelling thousands of miles by plane, leaving the Canadian panorama of mountains and rivers for this Scottish background, she was discovering to her surprise that it was very similar, though on a smaller scale.

She was still recovering from the shock of seeing Duncan again, but consoled herself that just as she was wondering what he was doing at the airport, having obviously come in on the scheduled flight from Heathrow, so he must be feeling the same incredulity on seeing her arrive on the Air Canada jet when, as far as she knew, he didn't even know that she had been in Canada.

Taking off in a small plane for an unknown destination was also puzzling. Was he visiting his parents? But surely Glasgow would have been nearer. All the way across the hundreds of miles of white ice floes she had thought of him at the hospital, traversing the wards; the same routine—and going back to his flat each evening.

Too much had been remembered in that moment when his eyes met hers across that unfamiliar foyer, with all the noise and hurrying passengers. Just two people for whom a short while ago time had stood still as they discovered their overwhelming love for each other. Now—the void between them had nothing to do with distance; the pain had been revived by his scathing look. It was all so terribly unfair. Couldn't he see that he might be in the wrong? Her eyes filled with tears, blurring the view of Ben Nevis, as the train wound around the straggling foothills. She blinked them away before the other passenger, an older man, scribbling away opposite her, could look up and notice them. It was all too much coming at the end of her traumatic journey, wishing that Duncan could be there to meet her, only to have that wish realised and then watch him disappear again. Only he hadn't been meeting her, she brooded, just passing through. But what strange quirk of fate had arranged it to be at the very moment?

And that look, the frown which had accompanied it, cutting her through with his unapproachable aura. Heavens—hadn't they worked together? Even that fact should have broken through. Just good manners—but to turn his back and walk away . . .

Anger possessed her then. A good, righteous anger which brought the flashing green lights to her eyes in the late afternoon sun. Just how dared he behave like that—in that holier-than-thou manner? It was time someone told him the truth about his own weakness, if that was what it was. Or perhaps he knew that he had lost her because of it and the derision was aimed at himself. She would never know. Her own resentment abated as quickly as it had flared, leaving the familiar ache in her throat as she realised that he couldn't know there had been no-one else in her life since he had gone out of it. And Sean's possessive behaviour was very much on the surface, which of course he had taken at face value. She couldn't blame him for thinking that everything was exactly the same. That even if he still loved her, so apparently did a few other men when each time he saw her she was with a different one. She gave herself up then to the discovery of the enthralling scenery around Fort William and as the train threaded beside the loch, she leaned forward, her face showing a little apprehension because, although it was summertime, she wanted to arrive at her aunt's croft before nightfall and she had no idea how much longer she would be travelling.

When the sea came into view and she saw islands dotted about, she was sure it couldn't be much further and it was then that her travelling companion opposite put his notebook away and said informatively, 'The Sound of Sleat—we're almost there now.'

'Oh—thank you. I was wondering how much further. You see, it's all new territory for me.'

'You're crossing to Skye, I expect.'

'Yes. Are you?'

He nodded. 'I have a cottage overlooking Tarskavaig Bay. This scenery around Arisaig just has to be out of this world though. I always enjoy coming back to it.'

She discovered that he was a writer but, what was more important, that he could advise her about getting to Aunt Bea's croft, way over in the Cuillin Hills.

Leaving the train, they crossed the Sound on the ferry and as it neared the bay and she saw the castle and woodlands on the hill overlooking it, she found a fresh spurt of energy. It all looked very exciting on that lovely summer day. Picking up her bags she went ashore to begin the last stage of her journey. Her companion couldn't be of much help because his route was across country although his car was waiting for him. But he did arrange for the taxi by the pier to drive her right to the croft once she had given the postal address.

'There is a bus . . .' the driver said, 'but I'm thinking you've missed it for today. Now, if you had come from Inverness, then you could have come across the Kyle of Lochalsh and found yourself a deal nearer to the village.'

'But I've come from Prestwick—and Inverness would surely have been right out of my way.'

'Aye,' he agreed as the car sped up the hill past the castle 'where . . .' he informed her, 'the Laird still lives—when he's here,' and then they were both silent as he drove along the winding roads towards the hills in the distance.

At last, having seen only isolated crofts or a hotel on the edge of a loch or hill, they came to a more built-up area, a general store and a few shops in the main street and, on the other side, a familiar sign 'Hospital'. They had passed an airstrip a little way back too.

This, she decided, was going to be one very expensive way of reaching Aunt Bea's croft, but there was no alternative and as the car began to purr through some very lonely country roads winding up over the heath, she really began to wonder how Aunt Bea had survived, imagining the sheer desolation in winter, as her eyes searched for some habitation more than just a croft tucked into the hills.

'It's a lovely evening,' she began, hoping that her driver would volunteer some information.

'Aye. *He breach.*'

Which, she discovered later, meant, 'It is fine . . .'

So—she might as well now have been in a foreign country, and an isolated one at that.

'It can't be much farther . . .' she said at last.

'*Ha nyall.*'

She eyed him surreptitiously. Was he simply showing off his Gaelic, or was he not aware that she didn't understand?

'How far?' she asked firmly.

He didn't reply, but as they rounded the bend and before them stretched a grassy road leading to the green covered hills, he pointed to a few scattered crofts a little way up. The car was already stopping.

Seeing her surprised look, he explained in English.

'It will be one of those cottages—you should ask in here.'

'Here' was a post office-cum-shop—in the front room of the croft nearest them. Meryl paid him and found herself with her two cases standing on the green path. She was conscious of the birds singing in every tree around her, the gurgling water in the stream as it hastened over the stones and ran under the small footbridge leading up to the crofts. The water was very blue, so was the sky. The purple hills beyond were blue—and all around her the trees were so fresh and green and the air so pure she felt almost intoxicated as she breathed in deeply. She was directed to the third cottage 'when you get up to the ridge' by the woman in the tiny post office; and picking up her two cases she resolutely walked up the narrow lane, aware of the curious glances from the inhabitants in the cottages as she passed. But no-one said anything, although she smiled shyly at them.

And then she was at the gate of Aunt Bea's croft. And she was there, sitting in the porch in the warm sun, perhaps looking out for her. But her aunt must have been dozing and didn't hear her approach up the flagged path between grass lawns which badly needed cutting, until she said her name very softly.

'Aunt Bea—it's me—Meryl.'

How ill her aunt looked. Meryl was shocked, having to mask her consternation quickly as the eyes opened and recognised her and tremblingly welcomed the girl who had come so far. Amid tears, and with Meryl's strong young arms to help her, they went into the house where even on this warm day a peat fire smouldered in the hearth. The room brought back memories of the home to which Meryl had come from school, the photographs and ornaments and pictures had survived, but something was missing. Yet the thick walls and low ceilings were homely and the room smelled of polish and the brass and copper shone, as it always had.

But her aunt was so changed in appearance that she hardly recognised her. Gone the rosy cheeks and brown thick hair of the Cornish woman who had left to come to Scotland several years earlier. Instead, she had become thin, her hair grey and her eyes sunk into her head. And she couldn't walk properly but hung on to chairs to support herself. Now she sat with her hands clasped in her lap, the skin, paper thin over her cheek bones.

Her whole appearance sent a shiver of apprehension through Meryl, the nurse in her recognising that there had to be more than grief to cause this collapse. She seemed almost too weak to talk, content to listen while her niece filled her in about the journey. In the old days, Aunt Bea would have bustled around putting on the kettle for tea, bringing out her home-made cakes and scones and home-made jam topped with cream. But she hadn't even suggested making tea—or anything else; but just sat there, fighting back her tears.

So Meryl took over, preparing a light meal for them both, suspecting that Aunt Bea hadn't eaten that day. Later she knew that she couldn't tolerate food: that she was very ill indeed. But the rest of that evening was spent in finding where everything was kept and helping her aunt to bed in one of the two bedrooms which had been converted from the original byre used for the animals during the long winters and for storing vegetables and straw. Now, with whitewashed walls and a new ceiling under the rafters, it was a true crofter's bedroom.

She noticed that her aunt flinched with pain and didn't finish her tea. But she wouldn't question her tonight, only observe. Perhaps tomorrow she could insist on her seeing her doctor.

'It's good to have you here, Meryl,' she whispered, when she was in bed.

Her niece bent to kiss her, squeezing her hand. 'Good to be here, Aunt Bea, and now that I am you are going to have a rest. Don't worry about a thing. I'll get breakfast in the morning and bring you yours in bed.'

Even her aunt's voice had changed, Meryl thought worriedly, as she undressed and slipped into her house coat. Then, taking a pair of white linen sheets from a drawer which smelled faintly of lavender, and some yellow fluffy blankets from the lower one, she made up her bed and, getting into it, lay looking up at the moonlight, fitfully patterning the ceiling.

But sleep evaded her. Instead, her brain reeled with the events leading up to her being here. Her fingers clenched in a spasm of pain as she remembered Duncan and the way he had turned away from her mute appeal to cross the floor to her. It all seemed so long ago, the hospital routine they had shared, disciplined and exciting because he had been there. The strength of their love which had grown and blossomed into passionate need. His rejection of her, devastating in its suddenness, the derisive words he had used to crucify her. And now, today, actually seeing him a few yards from her, watching with new despair as once again he went out of her life. She still loved him; nothing had changed.

But her aunt posed a new problem and one that could greatly affect her own plans for the next weeks, or longer. She was just very glad that she had come. She was obviously badly needed here in this white Hebridean croft.

Exhausted beyond conscious thought, she drifted at last into sleep, wakening to the sound of swallows chattering outside the tiny window and the sunshine streaming into her room.

Pushing her feet into slippers, she softly undid the latch on her door. Her aunt was still asleep.

While she waited for the kettle to boil, she put out teacups and milk and standing at the open door looking across at the Cuillin Hills, pink tipped in the morning sun, casting shadows of light and shade at their summit. It was beautiful.

Her aunt was awake when she carried in the tea and, curling up on her bed, she thought that she looked even more fragile in the early light. Today they could talk. Time to catch up on the lapsed months and years. She told her everything that had happened since they had left Cornwall. Except Duncan.

Meryl knew how carefully she must suggest that her aunt seek medical advice. When she tried to get out of bed her face was suffused with pain and she almost passed out.

Deftly, Meryl tucked her in again, brushing aside her protestations.

'You forget that I'm a qualified nurse, Aunt Bea,' she told her firmly.

'But . . .'

'Just tell me—where is the pain?'

'I don't know—my back, I suppose. But here too—it's—becoming unbearable . . .'

'I can see that. Does your doctor know?'

She shook her head. 'What can he do—at my age?'

'That has nothing to do with it. You're not more than your early sixties—are you?'

'Just sixty-one.'

'Good heavens. Still young.' She regarded her seriously. 'I'll have to call in the doctor—you know that, don't you? This can't go on. You're not eating, are you?'

'No. Food doesn't agree with me somehow.'

'There have to be tests,' Meryl said gently. 'I'm not a doctor—but pain is a symptom and should be investigated.'

'I'm not going to hospital. That's what happened when Lewis was ill, and he died there.'

'Oh—Aunt Bea—you may not need hospital treatment. And in any case, I'll stay until you're better. Now, where is your doctor's phone number?'

'You'll have to call the nurse first and she decides if you need him.'

'I am a nurse,' Meryl said patiently, 'and I think you do. What is his name?'

'Dr Collard. He'll be at his surgery.'

Without telling Aunt Bea, Meryl went down to the post office and phoned the surgery, giving a full explanation and her own qualifications to the practitioner when she was put through to him, which she had insisted upon.

He sounded nice, promising to come during the afternoon and, with this, Meryl had to be content.

'Don't you have any friends or neighbours to come in, Aunt Bea?' she asked when she got back.

'Morag brings my pension up to me and one or two women drop in from time to time.'

'But your food shopping?'

'The mobile van comes on Fridays. I manage.'

'And haven't you told anyone about the pain?'

'Oh, dear me, no. Just that I'm feeling a bit off colour.'

'Well—I've phoned the doctor and he's coming to see you this afternoon, so just rest and don't worry. I'm here—if you want me.'

She busied herself about the little house and washed a few things that had accumulated and after lunch watched for the doctor's car to come up the incline.

Used to dealing with doctors of every rank, she was able to ask his outright opinion after a protracted examination of his patient, helped by Meryl, and because he knew that she was an SRN, he spoke very plainly to her in the little room outside.

'I don't want to move her,' he began, 'but I want her to see a consultant right away. There seems to be some spinal collapse and other manifestations which bother me.' He looked grave.

'I understand, Dr Collard,' Meryl said quietly.

'I'll have a word in the right ear and see what I can do,' he went on. 'But perhaps you should expect him to come any time.'

'I will pay his fee if you can get a private consultation,' Meryl assured him. 'If it could be soon . . .'

'Leave it with me. Meanwhile—keep her in bed. She is very fortunate to have you here with her. I do wish she had called me in before this, but isn't that typical of these independent folk?'

At least something had been accomplished and this she confirmed in a letter to her stepmother that evening. Next day, she washed Aunt Bea and made her comfortable, not wanting to give her any sedation until she had seen the specialist and not knowing when he might come. It was a long drive from the hospital, if that was where he was. Nothing was the same on this Hebridean island. One had to go over to the mainland for more specialised care and major operations, it seemed.

She was cutting some of the pink roses which climbed up the white cottage wall just after lunch when she became aware of a grey Fiesta stopping at the gate. The car looked almost too small for a consultant's car and she wondered who else had come visiting.

Until the sun caught the familiar reddish tints in his brown hair when he climbed out and straightened his back. Her heart seemed to turn over; it couldn't be Duncan—impossible! But all her senses confirmed that it was, even before he reached for his medical bag and turned towards the little white gate.

She still stood transfixed, one hand pressed to her mouth as he glanced briefly at the croft to check that it was the right one. Then, as she came from the shelter of the rowan tree, he saw her. He couldn't fail to see her green eyes, moist with emotion, her hair damply curling into her neck and wearing no make-up—looking as fresh as he remembered her at the hospital. Only, today she wore a cool, yellow dress; her hands clutching the pink roses against her breast as if to still the thumping of her heart.

He regarded her gravely, his eyes sweeping over her uncomprehendingly while he walked slowly up the path.

'I hope . . .' he said quietly, 'you have some explanation, Meryl. I came here expecting to see a patient of Dr Collard. What are you doing here?'

'My aunt is your patient, Duncan,' she said bravely, 'and, believe me, I had no idea you were anywhere near Skye. Only that I was to expect a consultant. I don't understand why you have come.'

'I'm standing in at the hospital for six months before taking up a consultancy in London. Does that satisfy you as to my status?'

'You know I didn't mean that. I'm just so surprised that you're here and not at the hospital still.'

'Tell me about your aunt.'

'When I arrived two days ago I found her seriously ill.' Her voice cracked but she went on. 'Apparently, she wouldn't have medical advice and now I'm afraid it could be rather late.'

'Shall we go inside?' he said in a low voice.

She led the way noticing him having to lower his head going through the doorways. He spoke gently to Aunt Bea lying nervously waiting on her pillow. And Meryl fell in love with him all over again then as she watched his unhurried procedure, helping him at the right moments, sharing her aunt's pain too as he carried out his very thorough examination of her. Then he straightened up and sat down on her bed, telling her firmly but kindly that he would like her to come into hospital for a few days for further investigations and X-rays.

Perhaps because of her pain and weakness she no longer protested, or because she had faith in this tall, competent surgeon who assured her that he would take care of her himself and left, after pressing her hand comfortingly.

Following Meryl out to the kitchen where he scrubbed his hands in a bowl of soft, boiled spring water which she had put ready on a white towel on the table, he didn't speak at once. She waited, used to this short thinking time before he gave a decision. While he dried his hands he looked across at her. 'You suspect what is wrong, don't you?'

'I—think so. It's her spine . . .'

'Much more widespread, I'm afraid. There is very little I can do, but we'll know more after some X-rays, of course. At least—she can have the sedation she needs. Will you be staying on here for a time?'

'Oh, yes. I can't leave her now.'

'Are you alone here?'

'Yes. Why shouldn't I be?'

He raised his eyebrows. 'I should have thought it was an obvious assumption. You weren't alone at Prestwick—I assumed you came in with that Canadian. Didn't you?'

'Yes. I did. I was staying with friends of his over there.

I—took a patient over from my stepmother's rest home.'

'I see.'

'You don't, Duncan. But all this has nothing to do with the more serious situation I'm now involved in,' she said miserably. 'Except that I'm very grateful you are her doctor. She obviously likes you very much.'

'I'll send an ambulance out for her. Perhaps you'll come in with her.'

'Of course. Thank you.'

Refusing coffee, he said that he must get back to the hospital. He had patients to see later that afternoon. But she saw some hesitation in his manner as he stood framed in the porch, as if he wanted to say something more to her but then, giving her rather a strange look, he turned and walked decisively down the path to his car. She didn't move until it was out of sight, then went back inside, believing at last in miracles as she began to clear away the proof that he was actually here in her aunt's kitchen.

The reason for his visit saddened her again. She dared not think of the coming weeks, only that she had given her promise to stay, no matter what lay ahead. Besides, there were more immediate preparations to make before the ambulance arrived and her aunt needed some moral support and all the help she could give her. She found her trembling and cold with nervous anticipation of her journey to the hospital.

'You are coming with me?'

'Of course I am.'

'I—used to pretend you were the daughter I never had.'

'Oh—Aunt Bea. You were always like a mother to me when I was small.'

'I wish you didn't have to find me like this.'

'Look, I wish you had told me you were not well. But

I'm here now, and I shall stay.' Her throat constricted
and she had to turn her head away before she murmured, 'for as long as you need me . . .' Did her aunt
know how ill she was? And that she wouldn't be needed
for very much longer?

When the ambulance turned into the hospital drive-
way and stopped in front of the entrance doors, Meryl
saw Duncan's grey Fiesta parked in one of the lots. So he
was still here. How ironic these circumstances which had
brought them together under one roof again.

Strange too, as she went along the corridors behind
the trolley carrying her aunt into admission and later to a
room at the end where she would be on her own. She
even helped get her into the freshly-laundered bed and
put the roses she had cut that day into water, arranging
them on her locker where she would see them.

When the house doctor arrived to take notes she got
up to leave, having a word with the Sister on her way out
and promising to return next day.

She was surprised to find a message for her at reception asking her to wait as Dr Heyer wanted to see her.

She sat down on a chair feeling bemused, aware now
of an enveloping feeling of exhaustion, both mentally
and physically; anxiety and the trauma of meeting up
with Duncan again combined, leaving her no more inner
resources on which to draw. She sat, as if in a dream,
waiting for his door to open and for Duncan to emerge.
The sounds and smells and the environment going on all
around her were the ones she knew. The hospital was
small, almost like a cottage hospital. It was unbelievable
that she was here at all. She closed her eyes and didn't
see Duncan leave his room and come along the corridor,
nor see the expression on his face before he said
her name and she became aware of him. She stood
up.

'You—wanted to see me . . .'

He nodded. 'How are you getting back to the croft?'

'I'm hoping there will be a bus.'

'I shouldn't think so. Not up there, at this time. I'll drive you.'

He began to walk ahead of her, not waiting for her protest and, like an automaton, she followed. Because it was a warm day he wore only a soft grey shirt and navy pants, his jacket slung over one arm. His figure brought on a sense of longing which ran along the nerves of her body. Oh—why couldn't she stop wanting him this way? Where was her pride? Oh—how she loved him. There would never be anyone else for her like this.

Unaware of her traumatic thoughts, he opened the car door, closing it after her and came round to slide into the seat beside her. She was so close she could smell his skin, bringing back more intimate recall.

Edging the car out into the road he turned towards the hills.

'I can't believe this is all happening,' she said weakly, glancing at his profile as she wondered what he was thinking.

'Because you are here, with me, or your aunt's illness?' he asked abruptly, not changing his expression or glancing at her.

'Both, I suppose.'

'How are you going to get in to the hospital for visiting?'

She let out a long sigh. 'I don't know yet. I'll have to find that out. You will tell me—as soon as you know— if . . .'

'Of course.' Then he went on. 'Does staying on here affect your immediate plans?'

'No. I don't have another hospital yet.'

'You could come into this one on a temporary basis.

There are a few vacancies, I believe. Think about it.'

'I—will,' she spoke consideringly. Why not? If Aunt Bea was going to stay there for a time it might be an excellent idea. And Duncan himself had suggested it.

When they stopped outside the small post office he was amused to see chickens wandering around in front of his car.

'Don't come any further,' she told him. 'I can easily walk up there. It was good of you to drive me back. Thank you.'

She dared not meet his eyes for he would see only longing there. And no way would she ever become that vulnerable again where he was concerned.

'I would like to say it was a pleasure, Meryl,' he smiled sardonically, leaning back to regard her under half-closed eyelids, 'but having made a firm decision never to become involved with you again, I won't. Goodnight. I will no doubt see you at the hospital tomorrow some-time.'

'Yes,' she replied coolly, as she opened her door and only sighing deeply when he turned and drove away. She refused to let him see how much his words cut into her. And after all, wasn't she struggling with the same problem? Hadn't she promised that she would never let him tear her apart, ever again?

It wasn't true, of course, because as she let herself into the quiet croft, cool in the early evening, the truth asserted itself in her mind and she knew that if he held out his arms to her she would run into them. She wanted nothing so much in this world more than to feel them closing strongly around her as they once had. But for now she had to be content. The impossible had happened. Today they had been together again. Maybe—divided by many things other than distance; but she must try to be patient because, if he still loved her, there would be a way and somehow he must discover the truth—that there had never been any other man in her life.

CHAPTER NINE

MERYL was up early the following morning. She had a strange day ahead. The events of the previous day came crowding back into her mind with a kind of unreality. She found it difficult to assimilate that she and Duncan had met and actually talked together, almost as they had done in the very beginning. Her heart leapt at the prospect of seeing him again, even under the shadowed circumstances of Aunt Bea's illness. Which made her impatient to get to the hospital, only she wasn't sure about the bus times.

Immediately the post office opened she went down to enquire.

'There'll be only the one,' the little post mistress told her when she explained that she must get to the hospital and why. 'Now—you'll pick it up at the crossroads. There's a hotel where the climbers stay at the foot of the hill near to the loch—you must have seen it when you came through.'

Meryl nodded. 'But that is at least two miles from here surely?'

'Three, most likely,' the post mistress said placidly, 'and you have just an hour if you want to be on it. You could take a short cut across the moors, but I'm thinking you'd be best to keep to the road.'

Murmuring her thanks Meryl ran back up to the croft, changing her summer sandals for thicker soled shoes, slipping her smarter sandals into her bag because the sun was already hot and she was wearing a sleeveless cotton dress. On second thoughts she grabbed her raincoat too, having been warned that sudden rain squalls came in from the sea and across the hills without warning. Then resolutely she set off, soon leaving the scattered croft cottages behind. She began the long trek up the road which wound over the lonely moors. Occasionally a car swished by, but mainly full of tourists, and no-one stopped to offer a lift.

A coach with sightseers gazing out of the windows from Portree suddenly materialised going in the opposite direction and leaving a loneliness one could actually feel as she hurried on. Now the only living things were sheep and cattle away on the hillsides and a pair of buzzards wheeling and swooping high in the sky. All around the heather was filled with buzzing as bees gathered in the first honey and a blue-feathered bird flew across in front of her. She could have delighted in the loneliness and beauty around her if a glance at her watch had not reminded her that she had just twenty minutes to make that hotel stop and, as yet, there was no sign of it.

Quickening her steps she began to climb again the winding road, relishing the soft wind on her flushed face and through her loose hair, when at last she reached the top. Now the road twisted downhill past peat trenches where the digging had already begun for next winter's fuel. She saw squares of peat stacked ready to be collected, just as they were outside her aunt's croft door. Here no-one would dream of taking someone else's peat: it was safe to leave it there like that.

Rounding some huge boulders she saw with relief the rooftops and chimneys of the hotel and now it came into view and the two elderly passengers who were also going on the bus.

She began to run then as it appeared over the crest of the hill and trundled to a stop, picking up the other passengers and waiting while she climbed breathlessly on board.

The woman she sat next to told her that the bus would return about six o'clock that evening. She, and most of the other passengers, were going on to the ferry and across to the Kyle of Lochalsh to shop or visit for the day. The two elderly people who had got on with her alighted at the hospital.

Clearly, Meryl thought as she went up the longish drive into the hospital, she would either have to be on that bus or find some other means of getting back. She didn't relish the prospect of that lonely trek back across the moors either. If she was to visit her aunt each day she must think about getting a bicycle or a lift from someone else coming in, perhaps.

Unless, as Duncan had tentatively suggested, she came to work at the hospital while they were temporarily understaffed. It would depend on whatever decisions were made about Aunt Bea's stay here, of course, but the idea of working near Duncan again definitely appealed to her and began to take root.

Several patients were sitting on the row of chairs waiting to see Dr Heyer or his registrar. At reception she asked if she might visit her aunt, but was directed to the ward sister first. It was all so familiar to her, this kind of procedure, and when Sister McPherson came to talk to her she explained that she was an SRN and understood the situation and that she was staying in her aunt's croft.

'She has been to X-Ray,' the sister said with her Scot's accent very pronounced, 'and she is now sedated, as you will see. Dr Heyer asked that you see him before you leave. He has clinic until twelve, but if you want to go before just tell his nurse that you are waiting. He insisted that he see you.'

'Oh—I'll wait, of course,' Meryl said quietly. 'If that's all right?'

'She's in seven—you can go in—though I doubt if she will really know you're there . . .'

Today Aunt Bea looked even more fragile, her skin almost transparent, and Meryl was even more apprehensive about the results of the X-ray plates which Duncan had probably seen already.

Aunt Bea roused and Meryl spoke to her reassuringly and she drifted into sleep again.

Going along to the coffee lounge run by the local hospital league of friends, she sat quietly thinking about whether or not she should ask for an appointment with Matron. Outside, the row of chairs was emptying and she went out to wait after explaining to Duncan's nurse that he wished to see her.

'Miss Summers? Yes, I know about that. I'll tell him you're here, if you'd just take a seat.' So she sat down once more.

A half hour went by before he was free. She went into his room, her heart beating very fast, and saw his eyes sweep over her cool striped cotton dress and sandals. He was, as she often thought of him, familiar in his unbuttoned white coat, waiting—while he indicated a chair.

'Sit down, Meryl. You've seen your aunt, I expect.' His voice was cool and guarded—but the look on his face told her more than he realised.

'Yes . . .' she answered carefully. 'She's asleep—I don't think she really knew I was there.'

'It's best—for her . . .' he said, sighing deeply, as he reached for the large envelope containing her X-rays. 'I think perhaps you should see these.'

Together they studied the dark patches and her throat constricted as she saw the indisputable evidence of damaged and abnormal tissues.

'As you can observe, the metastasis is very advanced; there is also some obstruction.'

It was what she had herself suspected yesterday.

He went on, 'I intend to operate first thing in the morning.'

Her eyes flew to meet his, then. She knew only too well the implications of his prognosis and what such surgery could mean. Also, what having to make this kind of decision did to him, or any other surgeon.

'She would never make the journey to the mainland,' he said quietly. 'I don't have any alternative if it means giving her another two or three months. There's just a chance of that. I'm sorry, Meryl.'

'Poor Aunt Bea.' She looked back at him with clouding eyes. 'Does she know?'

He shook his head. 'No. Only that we want to do some tests and that she will be anaesthetised. That, for the present, is really all she needs to know.'

'Yes.' Suddenly everything seemed strangely unreal: the room—the two of them being here together—everything. This scene—one she had experienced often before: the same words, only then they hadn't referred to someone belonging to her. Because they were talking about Aunt Bea she was hopelessly involved in every way; the only relative she had left in the world.

He was watching her face, the fleeting emotional reactions. She heard him ask quietly, 'Are you all right, Meryl?'

'Yes. May I stay here? I'd like to help if possible. There's no point in being at the croft.'

'I had a word with Matron yesterday. Why not go along and see her now? It's probably good therapy. You're going to have a difficult time ahead of you. It might help to take your mind off a few of the problems if you're working here.'

She met his eyes in a brief encounter. It was as if they were playing some kind of waiting game. She felt unsure of anything. But the circumstances were too painfully stark for it to be a game. Duncan was treading warily, unsure too about her, and determined not to put a foot out across the dividing line he had set himself.

She turned towards the door, looking back to find his eyes appraising her intently.

'Are you going to Matron now?'

'Yes', she answered briefly as she closed the door. Her feelings were in a turmoil. Lethargy pervaded all her limbs. Her world seemed to be exploding around her once again. Duncan—Aunt Bea—everything. It was probably the nearest she had been to hysteria in a mild form since the break up.

The trauma of the last few days all contributed to a situation which had built up, bringing no ordered planning of her future, when she seemed to be trying to find her way through a thick fog. And she needed Duncan, the man she had known and loved, so desperately. She needed his love, his strength, to feel his arms holding her as they once had. She couldn't bear the dividing line he had set up, turning the man back into the surgeon, in kind, but professional guise, but not the one she knew.

She was grasping at straws in hoping they might work together in the same hospital again.

In the cloakroom she let the water, soft and cold from the hills, run over her wrists and face. Then running a comb through her hair and putting on fresh lipstick, she surveyed her face in the glass. How tired she looked: thinner too. Gone the glow she had started to recapture in Canada. There was pain in her eyes—and stress lines around them now. Perhaps work was the answer. And she would be near Aunt Bea here, not all those miles away up in the hills, unable to reach her if . . .

But she refused to think of that. Pushing back her shoulders and with her head high she went along to

Matron's office and tapped on the outside door, and was told at once to 'Come in.'

The mellow Scot's voice seemed to match the woman who smiled as she went up to the desk.

'Miss Summers? Dr Heyer has just phoned to tell me you might be coming.'

A frilled cap topped the neat dark hair, pinned into a chignon, and she was much younger than Meryl had expected.

'Sit down. I understand you could come in on a temporary basis to help us out. We're desperately short of staff at the moment, with holidays and other factors. You're qualified, he tells me, and also that you were both at the same hospital. What a coincidence . . .'

'Yes, Matron. We were.' She refused to be drawn on that one, but stated her full qualifications and experience and ended by saying why she was here on Skye and how coming to work here meant that she could be near to her aunt.

'When could you start?'

'Tomorrow, if that would be possible.'

'My dear girl. I welcome you with open arms. You're just what we need. We're a small hospital with only one general surgeon, though Dr Heyer is specialising in orthopaedics, I know, but he too is only filling in until our surgeon gets back. As you probably know, all major surgicals are transferred either to Glasgow or Inverness. But we're often extremely busy here, especially now with so many visitors to the island.'

'Yes. I understand that.'

'So—you'll come in tomorrow. I'll have your room got ready. Uniform will be supplied, of course. You know the rest. Is there anything more you want to know?'

Meryl didn't think so.

'Very well. Report to me here at 8.30 a.m. I shall have

made arrangements as to your ward by then.' She referred to administration and left the office feeling that she was back in a slot she knew. And—she could help Aunt Bea, if only morally, over the next week or so.

Sitting beside the bed in her room, her aunt totally unaware that she was there, seemed a waste of time when she thought of the things there were to be done up at the croft before shutting it up for a period.

As she came out into the warmth of late afternoon, she realised that there was no bus until six, almost two hours. She went into the general store and bought a few things, checking that there would be no transport until then.

'No—the bus comes through about then. But just a moment . . .' she called to her husband in the back. 'Will you be going up to the hotel soon, Angus?'

'Aye.' He came into the shop giving Meryl a quick look. 'Why?'

His wife explained. 'I can give ye a lift. Aye—it's no bother . . .'

Feeling very relieved, Meryl followed him out to an estate car, the back loaded with stores and in thirty minutes they were drawing up at the hotel.

'Can you manage the rest of the way? I'm a bit pushed for time.'

'Of course I can, and thanks . . .'

At least she knew the way now and that after she reached the top of the first hill rise it was going to be downhill all the way. But luck was on her side. She had only gone a short way when a van drew up and a Gaelic voice asked if she would 'be liking a lift'.

He was, it seemed, a parcel delivery courier and when she got out at the tiny post office he told her that he would be back on that road in the morning.

'I'll come by at seven-thirty. I won't wait because the

others have to catch the ferry. But I'll look out for
you . . .'

Calling in at the post office she explained that she was
closing the croft until she had her off-duty days when she
would be back, and why.

The evening passed quickly as she swept and dusted
and tidied drawers and cupboards, feeling that she was
intruding on her aunt's private possessions but seeing no
alternative. And while she worked, thoughts of Duncan
filled her mind. She had thought that she was strong
where he was concerned; that it would be simple to
return to the doctor-nurse relationship that had started
way back, but there was nothing impersonal in the
tumult he caused through her whole body. The desolate
longing she felt, as if she were only half alive. Yet, he
simply accepted that they could be together but on a
more civilised, professional basis, as if their loving had
never been. Perhaps it was not the same for him. Not as
deep and committed. So—she had no alternative but to
accept this, go along with it, if her self-respect would let
her. Just be grateful to be near to him again, even under
the unhappy circumstances of her aunt's illness.

Tomorrow was going to be quite a day. Her first in
uniform again; a crucial one for Aunt Bea; and for
herself, there was no better way than getting back into a
working routine when helping and caring for others
might just help resolve the personal aspects of her own
life. She was young—she wanted a loving relationship
and happiness. Oh, God—the happiness they had found
together—how long ago it seemed now. How could the
joy of it all be cut down by his jealousy when he should
have known her better?

When her bag was packed ready, she decided to
follow Duncan's example and switch off. It wasn't easy,
but she was desperately tired. It had been a long day and

she slept deeply to wake at six. While she drank her tea she wondered how Aunt Bea was feeling and what time she would be going to theatre. She had a strong presentiment that today was going to be one she would not easily forget.

When the van drew up there were already four other passengers ensconced in the back among a collection of parcels and bags, fishing rods, baskets and ropes. But her benefactor had reserved the passenger seat for her.

When they stopped at the hospital he asked hopefully, 'Will you be wanting to be getting a lift back tonight, then?'

'No,' she said gratefully, 'but thanks for the offer. I'm staying here for a time. I'm a nurse . . .'

'Oh—well, I'll be looking out for you and you'll be welcome to sit up here beside me if I see you.'

'Thank you,' she said again, aware of the necks inside the van craning to see her and four pairs of eyes assessing her qualities, whether as a nurse or a female she didn't know. News travelled fast, that she did know, on the island and by evening it would be generally known and the whole community would be keeping an eye on the croft for her. She need have no fears. In fact, no-one ever locked their doors here, Aunt Bea had said, whether they were in or out of the house.

Inside the hospital a junior nurse took her to her room, plainly furnished but comfortable, and she had it to herself. She collected her uniform. Here the aprons and caps were of the starched kind which she rather liked and she had in her case her silver buckle and fob watch which she had taken to Canada with her.

Changing quickly it was soon pinned on to her apron and when her cap was also in place she reported to Matron's office. Here every detail of her appearance was approved as she came straight to the point.

'We desperately need a staff nurse on women's medical currently,' she said, 'so I'm putting you there with Sister McPherson who is over the moon at having you. Especially as you are capable of taking over in her absence. Are you happy about that?'

'Oh, yes, Matron.'

'Fine. Then I'll take you along there now.'

The wards were bright with summer flowers, the windows open, the paint white, and attractive curtains were drawn back around each bed, making it as pleasant a place to be in as possible. The hospital, although not modern by Meryl's previous one, was adequate. More of a country hospital atmosphere, she thought. The younger nurses were getting the beds made and after a few minutes of being shown around so that she was familar with the contents of cupboards, linen, instruments and especially the drugs locker, she asked when her aunt would be going to theatre.

She already liked the comfortably proportioned Scots Sister very much and now that she realised the relationship between Meryl and the patient in Ward Seven, she was very concerned.

'I didn't realise . . .' she murmured. 'Why don't you go and see her? I expect she is drowsy because she had her pre-med at eight-thirty and she was very tired before that. You do know what she's going to theatre for . . . ?'

'I'm afraid so. Dr Heyer showed me the plates,' she said sadly.

'Ah . . .' What else was there to say?

Her aunt didn't at first recognise her in nurses' uniform.

'Is it time to go, then?' she asked weakly.

'Not quite. It's me, Aunt Bea. I'm going to be here when you wake up and help look after you. I thought you'd like to know that.'

'Good—girl . . .' she murmured sleepily and as Meryl's hand held hers comfortingly she drifted back into a sedated sleep. Meryl felt the tears sting her eyes as she bent to kiss her, blinking them back as the rubber wheels of the trolley stopped outside her door.

Sister followed it in. 'I thought you might like to go along to theatre with her,' she suggested, handing her the folder containing all the relevant history notes.

'Yes. That was thoughtful of you.'

It was new territory for her, but once inside the swing doors and she had handed over to the theatre staff, she was able to look around, recognising the same kind of equipment and machinery she was used to. The anaesthetic machine was wheeled up. The anaesthetist wearing his green cap and gown came through from theatre sporting a blond handlebar moustache, his eyes twinkling at Meryl as he said gaily, 'Hullo—you're a new face.'

'Staff Nurse Summers,' she said quietly.

'Are you staying, Staff?'

'No. I have to get back.'

'Right. We'll make a start then—Dr Heyer is waiting.'

Checking his patient's pulse rate, he found a vein and gave his first injection and they were ready to go into the theatre. The doors flew open and the trolley, with the machine now attached, was wheeled in. She saw in that brief time Duncan, theatre garbed, his mask leaving only the blue-grey eyes she knew holding hers above the trolley; then an expression she hadn't seen for so long was there, one she dared not interpret, but apart from the element of surprise as they swept over her uniformed figure, he was conveying an unspoken message across the sterile space between them.

It had reached her heart, making it beat faster, as she turned and went out into the corridor. He wanted her to know that he understood how she was feeling and that he cared about that. If anyone could save Aunt Bea—it was he. So there was nothing to do but wait now.

A junior nurse had made coffee for Sister McPherson and herself and was directed to make up the post-operative bed for the patient's return.

'Which won't be until this evening, I expect,' Sister said, 'so it's best to put it out of your mind if you can. You've quite enough to contend with on your first day here.'

Which was good, sound advice and she was surprised how quickly she learned the patients' names, their treatment and where to find everything in the filing cabinets about their case histories, although it was natural her thoughts should fly to the theatre and what was going on there from time to time. Much too soon for news yet though, she thought, as she got a patient out into the chair beside her bed.

It was Sister McPherson who told her quietly that her aunt had not survived the operation after calling her into her office and closing the door so that they were alone.

'Oh—no . . .' Meryl sat down, absorbing the shock, yet fully aware that she had known it could happen. Her anguish was for Duncan too. He had known also, yet gone in, taking that chance.

'I've made some tea . . .' Sister's voice invaded her train of thought. 'Drink it, my lass, it will help. Would you like to go off now?'

Meryl shook her head. 'No. I'd prefer to stay on duty, Sister. I know there will be things to do later—that only I can do—but I think work is the best therapy at the moment. There is nothing more I can do for my aunt— I'm just glad that I could be with her up until the last—she didn't know anything . . .'

'If you feel like coping I had thought I would just go and see my mother for an hour or so this afternoon—but

I can cancel it if . . .'

'Oh, no—please go.'

'Well, she will be wondering where I've got to and you know how one feels—you think nobody cares when you get to her age.'

'Of course you must have time off. I'm better having something to do—and as I said—I can't help Aunt Bea—any more.'

During the afternoon Meryl had adjusted an intravenous drip for a patient, so immersed in her task that she didn't hear Duncan come quietly on to the ward. Until she heard his voice as he asked the woman in the first bed something.

He waited for her, seeing the unhappiness in the greyish-green eyes which he had seen flash jade green with passion, but were now drained of emotion as they looked back at him.

'Sister is . . .' she began. But he put a hand on her arm. 'It's you I came to see,' he said firmly. 'Shall we go into the office?'

There were two nurses on the ward so she went with him. He closed the door and came near her, looking down into her face.

'You know how sorry I am about your aunt,' he began. 'I thought you would want to know what happened.'

She nodded, 'Please . . .'

'There was nothing I could do. It was inoperable—the secondaries everywhere . . .'

'Oh—how dreadful.'

'I thought I could perhaps give her a few weeks. I'm sorry, Meryl. She simply collapsed on us. Believe me—it is better this way—for her.'

'I know. I was afraid of this. We were both much too late.'

She turned her head, not wanting him to see how near she was to tears and refusing to meet his concerned eyes.

But he tilted her chin and, with a muffled groan, put both arms around her, holding her close, pressing her head into the hollow below his shoulder.

Afterwards, she wondered what an intruder would have thought if, coming in unexpectedly, he had seen them, but at that moment it hadn't mattered. Only that he was there when she needed him, his strong arms comforting, giving her the strength to hold on to her self control and a dawning hope that he still loved and wanted her.

He put her gently away when footsteps warned of an approaching nurse. She was still trembling and he held on to her arm. 'Are you okay?'

She nodded, not meeting his eyes, and, opening the door, he heard her say formally, 'Do you want to speak to me, Nurse?' warning him that they were no longer alone. As she went to the desk to get the required forms for the nurse, she heard his steps on the quiet blue tiles in the corridor and the swing door swish behind him.

At six, when Sister and she had caught up with everything and supper was being served to the patients, she was free to go. She could go out if she wanted to, so after writing to Elizabeth she went to post her letter, knowing it couldn't go until the morning but glad of some fresh air and time in which to think about the arrangements she must make and when she could visit the cottage. From the call box she got through to Elizabeth and told her that Aunt Bea had died.

'Oh—you poor love. Can you cope?'

'I think so. I've explained in the letter what I'm doing at the hospital, and Elizabeth—Duncan is in residence there too. He operated today.'

'Truth is stranger than fiction, they say,' Elizabeth commented after her first surprise. 'I wish I could come but it's a bad time. I've got two patients who need quite concentrated nursing. When is the funeral?'

'I haven't got that far yet. I shall know by tomorrow. But, Elizabeth, there is no need. It's much too far and would take you a couple of days to get here. Please—don't try to do it.'

Just a handful of crofters stood by while Aunt Bea was buried beside her husband; and Meryl was alone, until Duncan drove up and came to stand beside her.

She felt his hand under her arm steadying her at the saddest moments, and afterwards he drove back to the hospital while she began the task of going through the croft.

It now belonged to her. Aunt Bea had left her everything she possessed and because she wanted to stay on at the hospital, especially while Duncan was there and could do so without losing her independence where he was concerned, she decided not to do anything about it yet but use it as her home for a time.

Duncan had still not made any move to put their relationship on a firmer footing two weeks later. In fact, she felt he was avoiding her. But it was her long weekend off duty and as she left the hospital with her overnight bag to get the bus she saw him getting into his car in the drive. At first she pretended not to notice him, feeling the colour rush to her face instead. But he got out and called her name, coming to ask if she would like to be taken somewhere.

'I'm going up to the croft—the bus leaves in a few minutes. I can manage, thanks.'

'Get in, Meryl—please. I want to talk to you. Away

from here. Come and have dinner with me. Then you can go to the croft if you want to.'

It was what she had longed to do. To be with him, as before; but still she hesitated, afraid of the pain when they had to part once more. Because she didn't understand what his thoughts were—what he wanted of her.

His eyes were pleading. She gave a tremulous smile and slid into her seat. He closed the door and came round, pushing his long legs down to the pedals, slamming his door and gliding out of the drive to take a road she hadn't traversed before, which led behind the hills. His thinly-clad thigh touched hers and she drew away slightly, her pulses racing.

Her heart was pounding under her cream silk suit jacket, the one she had worn home from Canada. She was the first to speak.

'Where are you taking me?'

'I've found a hotel where they do marvellous food. I think you'll enjoy it. I'm so glad you decided to come with me, Meryl. I think we should talk before you take off again, as I suppose you intend to once the business of the croft and your aunt's things are resolved.'

Her heart sank a degree or two. Was that all? Did he want only to talk?

His hands were steady on the wheel—she loved his hands, sensitive yet strong. She loved him; she would always love him. Surely he knew that but was simply choosing to believe that her love was given too easily and to more than one? This made her resentment return, but she was too happy for it to take root. After tonight she would know what was in his mind. Perhaps at last realise how wrong he had been to condemn her out of hand, believe that she could be guilty of deceiving him.

The road wound around the blue hills, a perfect natural colouring against the green moors and banks of the low burns where blue and white water rushed over the stones in its bed. And as they drove across a stone bridge, over the stream, she saw the white hotel among the trees in its lovely setting.

As they got out Meryl looked around at the tranquil beauty, breathing in the pure air of the summer evening.

'Oh—isn't this beautiful? What a lovely spot,' she said softly, her eyes glowing.

'I thought you'd like it.'

He had reserved a table for them and after sherry they went in to eat through five courses of superbly served food. Over that meal the doubts and inhibitions were swept away.

They were gentle with each other. There were too many sensitive wounds to gloss over lightly and a lot to re-discover. Neither was it definite that they were going to start again. This was a new beginning and knowing his arrogant nature, she knew that he would not begin again without some deep soul searching. He would have to know how she felt about him now also. Her reticence at not accepting his invitation immediately must have thrown him, if he was under the impression that he had only to lift a finger and she would come running.

But now, watching him across the table, her chin in her hand as she listened to his plans for his future, she knew that he had only to ask and she would go to the ends of the earth. Just to be with him. She hadn't felt so completely one whole person since their break-up.

'London?' she echoed.

'Yes. I'm taking up a consultancy at the Middlesex in October.'

'That's wonderful. I'm thrilled for you, Duncan. Shouldn't we drink to that?'

He reached across the table for her hand and she waited for his next words.

CHAPTER TEN

THE wine had relaxed them both during dinner and, having imparted his special news to Meryl, Duncan seemed to unbend in other ways too. An element of trust, of something which was getting better all the time, seemed to be taking them along on a new level. They were enjoying every moment of being together. It shone in her green eyes, meeting his without embarrassment across the table; in the softening of his chin, the tense lines disappearing as he laughed more easily. It was like falling in love all over again. And as they left, somewhere in one of the leisure rooms a Scotsman sang liltingly, 'Over the Sea to Skye' and Duncan explained, although she already knew, the origin of the song.

'Bonnie Prince Charlie escaped in a boat to the Island in the 1745 Rebellion,' he said. 'Did you know that?'

She nodded, her mouth curving into the smile he remembered. 'Yes. With Flora Macdonald, wasn't it? Didn't she lend him a dress or something, disguising him as a woman?'

'So the story goes. I can well believe it. The whole island is tempered with Norse and Celtic folk lore. It seems a great many battles were fought here; invasion from English kings. They've always been fighting men. I think one can feel something of its history in the castle ruins and battle sites. But it's an island of great natural beauty and I hope I shall come again some time.'

'You're a true Scotsman,' she said happily as they came out into the golden summer evening. 'I'd like to have the time to tour leisurely around the coast too.

Maybe sometime I shall, because Aunt Bea has left her croft to me. For the first time, I really do have a home of my own.'

She looked pensively across at the hills, thinking of the aunt who had lived here in this majestic but lonely place, when all the time her heart was really in Cornwall which probably Uncle Lewis never even suspected.

Duncan was asking, 'Do you intend to live here?'

'I shouldn't think so. I might just let it out for a summer holiday home. I don't know—it's too soon to make those kind of decisions, I think.'

She didn't say that because of his new post in a London hospital she hoped it would have some bearing on her own plans. Because she wouldn't want to stay here after he had gone.

It was as the car was climbing up the incline to the croft that Duncan, who had been staring straight ahead and had not spoken for a while, now remarked seriously, 'Speaking of decisions, Meryl—I think we have to make up our minds about us—don't you?'

When she didn't reply, simply because she was taken by surprise and couldn't find words, he asked, 'Can I come in for a while?'

'Of course.' Her heart was beating very fast as he followed her into the cool darkness of the living-room.

'Sit down. I'll get some coffee.' Even her voice was a little unsteady; as she turned to go he reached for her hand, pulling her back and looking up at her.

'The coffee can wait—stop being so practical. I think I've said that before, haven't I? Let me say what I have to before . . .' He stood up, coming close to her.

'Before what?' she murmured, his nearness, the male scent of him in this intensely new proximity sending a delicious shiver of anticipation through her body as he turned her slowly to face him. She could feel his breath in her ear, on her face, and the contours of his body through her dress.

'Before this . . .' he said roughly, as his lips brushed her cheek before reaching her lips, closing over them in the way she knew. The magic was still there, binding them both in the fusion of rising, tingling, sensational warmth which made their breathing deepen and her arms involuntarily go up around the back of his head, drawing him to her in a desperate need to be part of him. So close—she felt like a homing pigeon returning to the place it belonged—as his arms tightened.

Then, even while her senses were still spinning in the breathless moment of wondering what was next, he lifted her arms down and put her firmly away from him. Then, thrusting his hands into his trouser pockets, avoiding the bewildered look in her eyes, he walked over to the small window, his back to her now. He didn't see the threat of tears.

She went silently through to the kitchen, automatically filling the kettle and switching it on, her legs weak and unsteady. It was too emotional a time to recover from immediately. She had fallen yet again. Refusing even now to listen to the cool voice of reason, warning her to draw back before it was too late. She knew she was heading for more hurt, more pain, if she allowed her senses to blind her again. He would do exactly as he had before, if the situation arose. Was he suddenly remembering that night at the flat? What was he thinking as he stood there, silently staring out at the hills. What had he intended saying to her?

Watching him surreptitiously, she knew that he still wanted her, still loved her—his male passion had proved that. Why then had he walked away from her just now?

Pouring water on to the coffee brought a swift memory of that tiny kitchen at the flat the first night he had taken her there. Did he remember too? She heard him coming across the room behind her, raising her head but not looking round. She felt him lifting her hair from her neck, keeping quite still except for a quivering deep in her body at his touch. He pressed his lips to her neck then and, straightening up, turned her slowly round, his arms crushing her to him hungrily and found her mouth, unresisting, because no power on earth could make her push him away when she had ached for his kisses like this.

'You're the only woman capable of doing this to me,' he murmured when he could let her go. 'I'd meant to exercise more control,' he said ruefully as he drew her over to Aunt Bea's chintz-covered settee and threw himself down beside her. 'We have to talk as well as make love—you know that. But I get easily distracted, as you see. I still love you, darling, want you desperately ...'

'I know ...'

'But—I can't share you ...'

'Oh, Duncan ...' she said wearily—'if you don't know now that you've never had any reason to doubt me, then there is no point—and nothing more to say. How could I do anything to hurt us, look at any other man when I love you so very much?'

'Oh, my darling. I'm a jealous fool, I know. I'm so afraid of losing you, I suppose. I can't let you go a second time.'

'You don't have to,' she said simply. And remembering the coffee, left him to fetch it. But he had said what he came to say and left soon afterwards. She didn't mind. She would see him tomorrow. And she was happier than she had been for a very long time.

Yet, as she lay thinking about the evening before sleep came, she felt a little niggle of uncertainty creeping in.

Could this happiness last? It would have to prove itself—for both of them, before she could give herself up to Duncan's ultimate, glorious possession of her. She would not, this time, be rushed into wedding plans. But Duncan hadn't mentioned them either. Perhaps he too needed more certainty this time.

But it didn't spoil any of the off-duty times they spent together, exploring the island, the various castles, the tales of history and legend which Meryl found fascinating and Duncan took as a matter of course.

'I'm a Scot . . .' he said proudly.

'And I love your Scotland—especially these Hebridean Islands,' she told him. 'Besides, I have a vested interest here now.'

They found deserted beaches and tiny coves and lay for the whole of one nostalgically tender afternoon on the sandy beach of an isolated bay watching the seals playing on a small island a little way from the shore. Small silver fish swam in the shallow water, tickling their toes as they walked barefoot in the warm water. Abandoned and free from hospital smells and integrated responsibilities.

He threw off his shirt and lay beside her, their fingers intertwined. His body, the brown hair covering his chest, very male and appealing to her senses strongly as she put her face against it, loving him so. The clean, unpolluted air from the sea cooling their heated bodies and above, only the blue and white clouds mistily encircling the hills. They might have been alone on the whole island. And here, in the summer, the days never seemed to end, deluding one into a false timing, so that dawn came too quickly. But their off-duty time together was sparse and precious. Even so—there was still a reserve beyond which Duncan would not go.

He visited the ward on most days where she was now

completely integrated. On that particular day she was having to change her twenty-four hours off-duty time unexpectedly. He was in theatre so she left a note for him.

Hurrying to get the bus, she found it especially full of people returning from the ferry and the mainland, or working folk going home. The chattering and buzz of conversation went on over her head and she paid no particular attention to it until she heard the man in the seat behind relating an incident at the landing airstrip that afternoon.

'Aye, it was a single plane—private. I don't know how he made it. What a landing . . .'

'Is the plane still there then?'

'Aye. It couldna take off with a buckled wheel, could it? Besides, the young Canadian piloting it had to go visiting over in the Cuillins somewhere. He was just lucky to be going anywhere except to the hospital or the mortuary. Said he'd flown from Ayrshire—I wouldna have trusted him with a bicycle, let alone a plane.'

For a heart-stopping moment she thought it might have been Sean. But did he fly? She had no idea and refused now to panic.

Yet she was impatient for the bus to reach the crossroads, jumping off and almost running along the road up over the moors. This evening the whole landscape was changed, the sun hiding behind darkening rain clouds and the first heavy drops started to fall before she reached the croft.

If it was Sean, what would he do when he discovered she was not there? It was typical of him, that landing. He created diversions wherever he went, oblivious of other people's opinions of him. What Sean wanted he usually got, one way or another.

Relieved when she saw no sign of a car or any intima-

tion that he was around, she hurried up to the croft, very
white against the darkening hills. The roses still bloomed
on the walls and she felt a pang of sadness remembering
that first day when Aunt Bea had been sitting there in the
porch.

The door was on the latch. Someone had been there.

Sean lay fast asleep on the settee, his shoes on the
floor beside him, bright yellow socks strangely incon-
gruous on the pink flower-patterned settee.

'Sean—wake up,' Meryl demanded crossly. Blue eyes
lazily regarded her from under half-closed lids before he
realised that she was standing there looking down at
him. Then he leapt to his feet to embrace her, which she
deftly avoided, and his arms fell to his sides.

'What are you doing here?'

'What does it look like, Meryl? To see you, of course.
Gee—what a welcome. It sure isn't my day. Did you pass
that airstrip?'

'No. But I heard about it on the bus. You made quite
an impression in more ways than one. You really flew
here to see me?'

'What else? Do you know how long it's taken me to
talk my uncle round to letting me fly his plane? Where
were you anyway?'

'I'm working at the hospital. You should have written
or sent a telegram first. Do you want some coffee?'

'I could use a drink. Beer—or scotch preferably.'

She shook her head. 'Sorry—I don't have either.
Coffee it is . . .'

'Are you living here alone?' he asked as an afterthought.

She nodded, her eyes clouding over. 'My aunt died
just after I got here,' she told him while she unpacked
the few things she had bought at the store while she
waited for the bus. Which was just as well if he expected

some food before returning to . . . She spun round. 'Where are you staying tonight, Sean?'

He shrugged. 'I haven't thought yet. Some hotel, I guess, unless you're inviting me to stay here with you.'

'Which I am not. You'll have to go back to Broadford or Kyleakin—there are guest houses and hotels there. I expect you'll get fixed up. But you can't stay here.'

'I guess there wasn't much point in coming anyway. I just thought . . .' he came close behind her as she opened a kitchen wall cupboard for a tin of soup. She stood quite still, her arm suspended. He said softly, 'I thought you might have missed me a little bit, honey.'

'Move away, Sean,' she told him firmly, turning to face him; then gently, 'Look—I told you—I don't feel that way about you. You're wasting your time and I find it embarrassing.'

He gave a snort of disgust. 'Don't tell me it's that doctor guy still bugging you? Haven't you got over him yet? I guess it's you who is wasting your time, Meryl.'

She ignored this, asking teasingly, 'Didn't your cousin come up to expectations?' She was trying to get back on to less emotive ground.

'Got herself engaged to a guy who owns a castle no less,' he kicked an imaginary ball disgustedly. 'Wears a kilt when he comes to dinner. Guess I'll be going back home at the end of the month anyway. I was hoping to take you back with me. That's why I came here to the Island. I haven't got over you, honey—guess I never will.'

'Oh—come on . . .' she laughed lightly. 'Of course you will. There's nothing between us to get over, except in your mind.'

It had grown very dark outside, the clouds low and menacing, already raining quite hard. She was worried about transport back to the airstrip. Storms in the

Cuillins were more of a phenomenon than bursting rain clouds. Meryl had only experienced one but it had whipped up the loch water and swept through the hills, turning them into clouds of mist and angry coloured clouds with white froth pounding against the granite rocks.

'Sean—have you ordered a taxi?' she asked anxiously. 'We are in for some very bad weather.'

'So? We're okay here, aren't we?'

'You can't stay here. I'm sorry . . .'

'Too bad. You can't turn me out in this.' He gave her the full benefit of his disarming grin, white teeth gleaming in the half light.

She immediately flooded the room with a warm glow from the lamps on the low tables and drew the chintz curtains against the misty darkness outside, feeling frustrated and a little angry with him.

The wind rose, howling around the croft and sending blinding rain against the windows, rattling them unmercifully. Even the heavy door shuddered, so that Meryl had to bolt it to keep it closed. It was chilly inside the thick walls of the house and she hadn't thought to bring in dry twigs or peats. She felt restless and not quite in command of the unusual situation in which she found herself. Besides which—Sean seemed to be enjoying it. No phone—no outside contact. It was rather ludicrous.

Another strong gust of wind and rain slashed the windows and he sat down again, crossing his legs nonchalantly. 'There's no way a cab will come out for me tonight. I guess I'll just have to wait until morning,' he averred, smiling up at her with his head on one side irritatingly. 'I just wish you had a bottle of scotch in the cupboard though. It's diabolical to be right here where they distil the stuff and you're out of it. No beer either.'

She shook her head and left him to start supper,

breaking eggs into a pan for an omelette and grilling bacon. Then, slicing a home-baked loaf from the baker near the hospital, she set the table and all the time her uneasiness grew.

'I wasn't expecting you and there's only cheese and fruit afterwards. I'm not here very often to need fresh food in stock.'

'Okay,' he said, at last accepting that Meryl meant what she said and he wasn't going to have the cosy evening he had envisaged. That even with them both under the same roof she would probably lock her door. This was one girl he didn't break down easily. Some ice maiden—yet—how she turned him on. He was getting sore, watching her sullenly while she did the dishes. 'I guess I should have gone back before this weather started. What on earth do we do all evening?' He looked up hopefully. 'Any suggestions?'

'You're incorrigible. But you know, you have to go first thing in the morning, don't you?'

'Oh, sure. And as soon as that wheel is fixed I'll take off, believe me. I made some mistake in coming here.'

A new squall of wind and rain sent her to the window. Something had crashed outside but it was too dark to see anything. Even the hills were blotted out now.

Then, as she passed the settee, he grabbed her arm, pulling her down on to him. Caught off guard she lost her balance, struggling, held fast against his virile muscles; hurting her as his manhood and desires overruled his head. She was angry with herself now, as well as him, as she fought him off, flushed and unexpectedly near to tears. The noise of the storm outside reached a crescendo, a renewed gust shook the door almost as if someone was banging on it. It came again. Someone was.

Sean released her then, his face blotched with suppressed passion but for her it was the diversion she needed.

Sliding back the bolts the door was wrenched out of her hands by the force of the gale and by Duncan, water streaming from his oilskin, trying to get inside and shutting it again. Even then it took all his strength to get it shut and the bolts in place again.

'How on earth did you get through?' Meryl was so relieved to see him she forgot what his reaction to finding Sean there would be.

'I was out anyway so thought I may as well come on and see that you were all right. Not sure it was such a good idea though . . .'

Sean was still sprawled on the settee when she pushed open the door.

Duncan's brow creased as if he was in some physical pain. His jaw tensed and ignoring Sean's laconic, 'Hi, there,' he snapped, 'I see I needn't have bothered. So it was you on the airstrip today. I might have known.' He looked with hard eyes at Meryl. 'I suppose it was another of your innocent deceptions. When I asked you if you were still seeing each other—you told me you hadn't heard from your Canadian friend. So how did he know where to find you?'

She shook her head wordlessly, hearing the anger and pain in his voice. But for Sean it was a good moment to butt in, which he did with gusto, jumping to his feet.

'Hey—don't you speak to my girl like that.' He tried to put an arm around her shoulder protectively, until she stepped away. Duncan's oilskin had made a pool on the floor. He shrugged himself back into it and made a move towards the door.

'Please . . .' she implored. 'Duncan—please wait. I had no idea Sean was coming.'

He turned angrily. 'But he's here, Meryl, and he

obviously intends to stay the night. At your invitation, no doubt. For as long as you want, as far as we are concerned.'

'Please—wait . . .' she begged and if he had not been so blindly angry and disappointed he might have read what was in her eyes.

'Nothing,' he said acidly, 'would keep me here now.' The bolts undone, he strode out into the full force of the storm. She saw the blur of his car at the gate as Sean came to help her get the door closed again. Even so, she had to mop out the rain which had blown in, soaking her dress and hair.

Bedraggled and thoroughly miserable, she went into the bedroom, returning with blankets which she threw on to Aunt Bea's bed. Sean looked sullenly on. He knew now that she would never forgive what he had done. He wasn't sure he could forgive himself.

He heard the sob in her voice as she stood in the doorway. 'First thing in the morning I shall go to the post office and phone for a taxi to take you back to the airstrip and after that I never want to see you again. Sean, you have destroyed me tonight.'

'Gee—I'm sure sorry, Meryl. I mean that. But he'll be back—if he wants you—I know.'

'Not after tonight. You just don't understand, do you?' A sob shook her voice. 'I was happy again, for the first time—we were just getting back together again. I love him, Sean. You don't know the meaning of that, do you? I—think I hate you for what you've done.'

He was ready to believe that.

'And you didn't help.'

'No. I guess not. But I do have some excuse. I haven't got you out of my mind since I first saw you over at the Hunter place. Now—I guess I have to, so the sooner I take off—the better.'

'I agree.' She went into her room and he heard the latch slide into place.

The wind kept up and the rain beat on the windows relentlessly and it was almost dawn before she slept.

In the morning he had gone, leaving a note which read, 'Goodbye. I really am sorry. Sean.'

When she went to the post office to ask where she could find someone to repair the roof of the outhouse partly blown off in the storm, she asked if Sean had telephoned from there.

'No . . .' The post mistress gave her a curious look, 'but he was picked up around 7.30 when the van came through. Did he have a train to catch?'

'No . . .' she said absently, 'a plane.'

'A plane?'

'Yes. It was such a dreadful night he couldn't get back to the airstrip. I have to make it to the hospital this afternoon. Do you know of anyone going in; if not, I had better ask the taxi people to come out for me.'

'Oh, no. Today we close early and my sister and I are going over to the mainland after lunch. We will gladly take you with us, Nurse.'

Meryl thanked her. The hill up to the croft dragged at her legs today. But it was fine and warm and last night's storm which had caused so much havoc seemed hard to believe in the peace and tranquillity all around; the white crofts nestling among the green banks, except that the stream, swollen with rain from the hills, was rushing madly over the stones and the birds in the eaves were restless in the aftermath.

Meryl stood listlessly at the kitchen window, a cup of coffee in her hand, gazing out at the bedraggled garden. She had decided to shut up the croft and make further decisions about it later. She had no inclination to stay here now. It was time to go. She would ask to see Matron when she reached the hospital. The staff situation was improved and she had taken the post with full understanding that it was temporary.

Sighing heavily she packed away some of the things which wouldn't be needed if she decided to let it or shut it up for the winter. Now—all she wanted was to get away.

Matron raised no objection to her leaving at the end of the month, a few days away, waiving the statutory notice at Meryl's request.

So it was that she said goodbye to Sister McPherson who, while not wanting to lose her, noticed with concern the dark rings under her eyes. She also noticed the way her eyes flew to the swing doors each time someone came or went and that Dr. Heyer was not visiting as much as he had been. Matron had told her they knew each other before and it wasn't long before she drew her own conclusions.

Strange too that he should be going away for a couple of days just as the staff nurse was leaving. She imparted the information casually.

'Did you know that Dr Heyer has gone over to the mainland, Staff?'

Her head shot up. 'No. I—haven't seen him around.'

'He's gone up to Inverness to visit a patient we had here. Does he not know you're leaving then?'

Meryl shook her head. 'Maybe not. I haven't told him.'

'Aye, well—he'll be back tomorrow.'

So Duncan was avoiding her. She knew it for sure when he came into the ward the day after he was back, addressing himself only to Sister. That evening she made a long phone call to Elizabeth.

'I'm coming home . . .' What wonderful words they sounded. Elizabeth, wondering why she didn't mention

Duncan as she had in her letters, refrained from asking questions. But she had heard that lethargic note in Meryl's voice before, and wondered.

When Meryl left the hospital for the last time she still hadn't spoken to him alone. The following day she shut up the croft for the winter, undecided when she would return.

This time she had more luggage than she had arrived with and had to hire a taxi to take her through to Kyleakin and the ferry across to the Kyle of Lochalsh. Here she waited for the train to take her to Inverness where she had booked a sleeper berth to take her to London.

Her throat ached with the disappointment at not seeing him before she left. Not ever now—it was not likely their paths would cross again.

Sean's plane too was not on the airfield when she drove past. She had groaned inwardly then; did he realise the chaos he had brought into her life when he decided to fly back to England with her that day in Vancouver? Now he was out of her life for good— Duncan too.

Now she had to find a new sense of direction. But if they had to part she would have liked him to know that she had never deceived him in any way.

Tossing in her berth, listening to the wheels over tracks, watching the stations flash by, she arrived at King's Cross and embarked on the second stage of her journey later that morning to the West Country and home.

At King's Cross she had met a sister from her old hospital, married now and living in London. But there hadn't been much time to talk and she reminded her of Duncan anyway.

Home at last. Elizabeth was waiting at the station with

the car. That evening Meryl told her the whole story, or as much as she thought necessary.

'It's diabolical . . .' Elizabeth fumed. 'I've a good mind to write and tell him the truth myself. Who does he think he is? Of all the arrogant swines—he really is the worst kind.'

'No . . .' Meryl protested, 'he isn't at all like that really. He's kind and gentle and understanding. Just a little arrogant, I admit, but only when he's not sure of something and wants to cover his feelings. He was wonderful when Aunt Bea died. The funeral and afterwards. It's just that he has this terrible jealousy, as if he's afraid to trust any woman too much. And he does think I've let him down dreadfully. I know he loves me . . .'

'Really? Well he has a strange way of showing it. But you obviously do—love him, I mean.'

'Yes . . .' she admitted, 'It's not something that goes away, is it?' She took a deep breath. 'But it's over now, Elizabeth. I just have to live with it. Oh—it's so good to be here with you. Thanks for letting me talk it out. It has helped, really.'

'Just take one day at the time,' her stepmother advised sensibly. 'Meanwhile, you can help me with my two convalescents as soon as you feel rested. I might even take a day or two and leave you in charge, if you feel up to it. I want to do some shopping and—well—I do have a few decisions of my own to make up my mind about.'

Seeing the brightness in her eyes—noticing again the tell-tale bloom on her skin—her general glow, Meryl guessed rightly that it had something to do with the doctor who had been so attentive during the Christmas holiday.

'Yes . . .' Elizabeth said happily. 'He does want us to get married.'

'And you're going to say yes?'

'I don't think I can do anything else.'

'So—will you keep on the rest home?'

'For a time, yes, I think so. I can't unsettle my residents too much, but decisions will have to be made some time. They affect you too, as we are joint owners of this house.'

Early in September, Elizabeth and her doctor husband went off for a brief honeymoon touring France, leaving Meryl in charge. It was a busy and very responsible time for her and each night, leaving the night staff to cope, she fell into her bed and slept until morning. Duncan seemed a long way back. She no longer lay awake obsessively thinking about what might have been. It was over. Forget him. She never would. His influence on her emotions was too strong for that; but she had to get on with her own life now. She even wondered if she might take on the rest home, or help out with it so that Elizabeth might spend more time in her new home with her husband.

She was back from her honeymoon looking radiant but worried about Meryl.

'You're doing it all over again, aren't you?' she chided. 'You've lost weight—and all the life has gone out of you. And what for? A stupid man who can't even tell the difference between truth and fantasy.'

'Elizabeth, Duncan is a consultant . . .'

'And like a lot of clever people—he can't manage his own life, while dedicating it to others. Somebody always loses out.' Ignoring her protests, she insisted on Meryl going out for a breath of sea air. 'It's a lovely afternoon; go up over the cliffs and take in some good deep gulps—you're much too pale for my liking. I'll have tea ready when you get back. Cream scones with jam . . .'

'Oh—Elizabeth—you're wonderful. I might just do that. I do so love it up there. Thanks.'

Her eyes brightened with anticipation as she pulled on a yellow wool jacket and went out into the golden afternoon sunshine, then took the short cut leading up on to the grassy cliff top and made for her favourite cove. There, perched on top of a boulder, she watched the waves crashing against the rocks, sending up sprays of white foam, cascading off them to retreat into bubbling ripples over the white sand. Small boats with brightly coloured sails tossed fearlessly out there on the Atlantic waves and as she watched, Meryl knew that it was time to come to grips with her life, her future. She could no longer go on letting her emotions sap her energy, mentally and physically. She must make decisions and retrieve her sense of direction. Get on with her own career.

A sob rose unbidden to her throat and tears blurred the scene in front of her, but she fought them back, realising yet again how deeply the hurt was embedded. Duncan's distrust; his jealousy. Would he ever know just what he had done to them both? She would never know because it was unlikely she would ever see him again.

If only she could have known that at that very moment Duncan's car was threading its way through the narrow streets of the town and already turning to head up the hill towards the tree-lined avenue and Bay Trees.

He had arrived in the town after his long drive from London with no clue to her whereabouts, other than that she was at the rest home. But, searching through the telephone book, he ran his finger down the list of people named Summers.

Elizabeth, answering the phone in the middle of setting the tea trays, was surprised to hear a male voice with a Scot's accent asking very positively to speak to Meryl.

Explaining that her stepdaughter was out, he said,

'I'm Duncan Heyer and I've driven from London to see her. When will she be back?'

Elizabeth then directed him to the home and a few minutes later he was on the doorstep.

'You're not at all what I expected,' she told him in her lovely Cornish accent, as she opened the door. 'Come in—I've just made some tea. Meryl will be surprised, to say the least, Dr Heyer; but I'm glad you've come. I'm not sure what Meryl's reactions will be though.'

'I must talk to her. I only hope it isn't too late and that she will see me.'

'You have no-one but yourself to blame if she feels that it is too late,' Elizabeth said gravely. 'I know a little of what happened and you should know that there isn't an ounce of deception in my stepdaughter anywhere. I'm afraid she has been very unhappy.'

A shade of annoyance crossed his face as he stared out over the garden. 'I can explain . . .' he said briefly, 'but only to Meryl.' He turned to accept the cup of tea she passed to him. 'I'm sorry—but you do see that it is something which concerns only the two of us.'

'Yes. Of course. And when you've finished your tea I suggest you go out of that white gate at the end of the garden and take the path up over the cliff top and just look until you find her. Perhaps later you might like to come back for tea.'

She saw his attractive smile then as he hastily swallowed the tea and murmured his thanks and she watched his tall figure disappear through the gate and head for the cliffs

There were only a few scattered people about and she was not among them, so Duncan made for the headland. From there he could see both beaches.

Meryl, rested now, had to climb over the rocks to avoid being cut off by the in-coming tide and arrived breathless at the top just as he came round the headland. He saw her standing motionless looking out to sea, the wind blowing through her hair.

Her name escaped from his lips and she turned, almost as if she had heard. There was no mistaking those long, purposeful steps as he covered the green turf between them, nor the familiar set of his shoulders under the navy blazer and white roll-neck sweater.

She saw the wind teasing the red-brown hair as he drew near to her, standing quite still, scarcely able to believe that she was not dreaming. She felt her nerves tightening against this new and totally unexpected impact, calling up all her reserves, remembering the decisions she had just made. But none of that mattered when he reached her and, after looking deeply, searchingly into her green eyes, he groaned and took her into his arms, holding her close against his chest, his thudding heart, smoothing her hair as if she were a lost child found.

'Forgive me. It's the only thing that has to be put right, my darling. Before anything—can you forgive the hellish wrong I did to you? The, yes—unforgivable things I said—let myself believe. Sheer imagination—I know that now—oh, God—how did I make so many mistakes?'

His grip on her fingers tightened; but still she couldn't help him until gently he drew her down on to the grass beside him, still searching her eyes for the answer he needed.

'Say something, darling . . .' he begged. 'Nothing can erase the way I've behaved—how could I be so stupid—so blind? Can you forgive me? Understand why?'

'Forgiving is one thing—understanding why is quite another,' she said softly. 'Because I loved you so much I thought what we had far above that kind of deception and pain. You see, I trusted you and you had no reason to distrust anything I did—ever.'

'The night at the flat . . .' he began.

She broke in, 'Not only then, Duncan. When I got back from here—simply because someone got off the train with me, you jumped to all the wrong conclusions. And Sean—there were reasons behind his visit which you didn't even bother to find out about. I told you—he meant nothing . . .'

'I know . . .' he said in a low voice.

'And there will be other times . . .' she said sadly.

'Not when you belong to me . . .'

'Oh, Duncan, without complete trust—how can you expect any marriage to work? It would be like living on the edge of a volcano just waiting for an eruption,' she shuddered. 'That evening at the flat when you deliberately misinterpreted what you saw. Why didn't you let me explain? It was so simple—so innocent.'

'Don't . . .' he begged. 'I know that now. That's why I'm here.'

'Oh?'

'That night—I just took everything at face value—as I saw it in that brief moment—you, flushed and so lovely, making me want you desperately—and then that houseman looking—well, you know the rest.'

'But how . . . ?'

'How do I know what really happened? As you know, I'm in London now—but last week I went back to attend the conference there at the Medical School and after one of the lectures I was approached by one young house-man demanding to speak to me in private. It seems he needed to get the whole thing off his mind once and for all. I—don't seem to have come out of this too well, do I? Is it too late, Meryl? Do I get another chance? For God's sake—I need it. I love you so very much—you are still the one girl for me—can we start all over?'

'Oh—Duncan . . .' her eyes were brimming now. He drew her closer, kissing away the tears, his voice husky with emotion as he said seriously,

'I can only promise to try to combat this stupid jealous trait of mine. I've given it a lot of thought—I know where it stems from, way back . . . Maybe it will be different now that I belatedly recognise it for what it is.'

Compassion flooded her. 'I love you . . .' she said simply, 'and I understand now.'

With his kiss came a return of the warmth and passion which had bound them together from the beginning. Her feelings, so long starved, pulsed and leapt to answer his in an elemental desire which drove out everything but the fact that he had come to her; the love they shared even more precious now.

He stood up, pulling her gently to her feet, looking down at her with such an expression of love which only she had ever seen on his face. 'You are going to marry me—aren't you? Soon?'

Her eyes were like emeralds in the autumn sunshine.

'Yes—oh, yes . . .'

He kissed her eyes, the joy of it almost too much to bear—even for him.

'In which case . . .' he said firmly as they began to walk, hand in hand, back towards the house, 'we have to do something about a honeymoon or whatever. I have three weeks before taking up my new appointment in

London. And we have to find somewhere to live, my sweet. Do you think you can make it?'

Meryl nodded happily, tears on her lashes still unashamedly clinging there.

'We can do anything as long as we are together—you know that,' she mused, 'and we do have a life time to do it in.'

The wind blew her hair across her face and he involuntarily pulled her close again, turning her to face him.

'Oh, Meryl—I want you so much . . .' he said huskily. 'I need you in my life—with me always—at the end of the day.'

'And I you,' she said simply.

Elizabeth was patiently waiting for their return. She had no illusions about the outcome once she had seen and talked with Duncan, and over scones and strawberry jam and cream some of the arrangements began to take shape for their wedding.

Duncan stayed that night, returning to London next day to make further plans for his parents to come to London, and a week later Elizabeth and Meryl travelled to London to meet them and book in at an hotel for the marriage the following day.

On the plane taking them to Cyprus on the first stage of their honeymoon, Meryl decided that she could never hope to be this happy ever again. It was almost too perfect. With Duncan beside her their future assured to share—and the heartaches of the past months just a memory.

'What are you smiling about so secretively?' he asked softly.

'Just thoughts . . .' she whispered back.

But she was remembering one of Aunt Bea's expressions, that 'Love will always find a way.' How right she had been and Duncan, here beside her, to prove it. One day they must go back to that cottage on Skye again and make new memories within its walls. But now—they were on their way—to make other, more precious memories.

Doctor Nurse Romances

Doctor Nurse Romances

Romance in modern medical life

Read more about the lives and loves of doctors and nurses in the fascinatingly different backgrounds of contemporary medicine. These are the three Doctor Nurse romances to look out for next month.

FLYAWAY SISTER
Lisa Cooper

TROPICAL NURSE
Margaret Barker

LADY IN HARLEY STREET
Anne Vinton

Buy them from your usual paperback stockist, or write to: Mills & Boon Reader Service, P.O. Box 236, Thornton Rd, Croydon, Surrey CR9 3RU, England. Readers in South Africa-write to: Mills & Boon Reader Service of Southern Africa, Private Bag X3010, Randburg, 2125.

Mills & Boon

the rose of romance